For Maggie

PENGUIN BOOKS

THE LOVE HEXAGON

William Sutcliffe was born in 1971 in London. He is the author of two other novels, *New Boy* and *Are You Experienced?*, both published by Penguin. His books have been translated into twelve languages.

The Love Hexagon | William Sutcliffe

PENGUIN BOOKS

PENGUIN BOOKS

Published by the Penguin Group
Penguin Books Ltd, 27 Wrights Lane, London W8 5TZ, England
Penguin Putnam Inc., 375 Hudson Street, New York, New York 10014, USA
Penguin Books Australia Ltd, Ringwood, Victoria, Australia
Penguin Books Canada Ltd, 10 Alcorn Avenue, Toronto, Ontario, Canada M4V 3B2
Penguin Books India (P) Ltd, 11 Community Centre, Panchsheel Park,
New Delhi – 110 017, India
Penguin Books (NZ) Ltd, Cnr Rosedale and Airborne Roads,
Albany, Auckland, New Zealand
Penguin Books (South Africa) (Pty) Ltd, 5 Watkins Street, Denver Ext 4,
Johannesburg 2094, South Africa

Penguin Books Ltd, Registered Offices: Harmondsworth, Middlesex, England

First published by Hamish Hamilton 2000
Published in Penguin Books 2000
1

Copyright © William Sutcliffe, 2000
All rights reserved

The moral right of the author has been asserted

Set in 11/14 pt Monotype Sabon
Typeset by Rowland Phototypesetting Ltd, Bury St Edmunds, Suffolk
Printed in England by Clays Ltd, St Ives plc

'The state of sexual bondage is, accordingly, far more frequent and more intense in women than in men, though it is true it occurs in the latter more often nowadays than it did in ancient times ... Many strange marriages and not a few tragic events – even some with far-reaching consequences – seem to owe their explanation to this origin.'

– Sigmund Freud, 'Contributions to the Psychology of Love' (1918)

'I did not know why, but her weeping made me want to hold her and fondle her breasts.'

– Paul Theroux, describing his friend's wife in *Sir Vidia's Shadow* (1998)

1

'There's nothing.'

'There must be something.'

'There's nothing.'

'What about on the top shelf?'

'The top shelf?'

'Yeah. At the top.'

'It's funny you should suggest that, 'cause I was planning to look at only the bottom two shelves. It hadn't occurred to me to look at the top shelf, at eye-level, where we keep all the food.'

'There's definitely something on the top shelf.'

'I told you. There's nothing. Just some eggs.'

Lisa walks into the kitchen, wearing socks, knickers and a bra. Mascara bottle in one hand and brush in the other, she stares at Guy.

'Nothing – just some eggs?' she says, blinking her lopsidedly coloured eyelashes.

Guy closes the fridge and stands up, holding the box of eggs.

'Yeah.'

They smile at one another.

'Poisonous eggs, or edible eggs?'

Guy opens the box and looks inside. 'Errr . . . they look relatively edible.'

'It's a crazy idea, but why don't we eat the eggs?' she says, wandering back to the bedroom.

'I'D ALREADY THOUGHT OF THAT!' he calls after her. 'YOU'RE ONE STEP BEHIND, MATE.'

Guy places the box on the kitchen working-surface and stares at the six pristine domes. Beautiful. How do chickens manage it? If I could lay eggs, he thinks, I'd die a happy man. Or a happy chicken. Assuming I was free-range.

'TWO OR THREE?' he shouts.

'WHAT ARE YOU DOING?'

'SCRAMBLED.'

'ONE AND A HALF.'

'ONE AND A HALF? THAT'S NO MEAL FOR A GROWING GIRL.'

'That's the whole point,' says Lisa, appearing in the kitchen again, now wearing socks, knickers, and a tight, spangly T-shirt. 'I want to be a non-growing girl.' She pinches a roll of flesh from the side of her bum and angles it accusingly towards Guy.

'You look fine. And why is it my fault?'

'You're always cooking.'

'If I didn't cook, we wouldn't eat,' he says, indignantly.

'Exactly. It's your fault.'

'You'd rather eat nothing?'

'I don't like scrambled, anyway.'

Lisa has a habit of changing subjects in the way most people change cable-TV channels. This was perhaps the most curious aspect of her relationship with Guy. While he could happily spend an entire weekend discussing, say, the use of voiceover in the final section of *Goodfellas*, Lisa, if called upon, could dispense with the nature of religion, the causes of war and the future of information technology in a matter of minutes.

Strangely, this fundamental inability to hold a conversation had served as the bedrock for a relationship which, after four and a half years, seemed as solid as ever. In place of genuine communication dealing with the subjects they most cared about, they managed to talk crap to one another round the clock and remain in serene happiness.

When they were together, neither of them had to perform. The public personae that constituted who they were in the eyes of their friends became irrelevant. Guy wasn't called on to listen to anyone's problems, Lisa didn't have to do anything outrageous or noisy, and for both of them this was an enormous relief. After all, living up to your personality is generally rather an effort, and alone together they simply didn't have to bother. Despite their wildly different natures, in private, the notion of separate personalities gradually slipped away as, over the years, they worked together at constructing a vast fortress of chat.

'I could do an omelette,' he says, veering on to the new subject with practised ease.

'OK. I'll have a two-er.'

She ambles back to the bedroom, while Guy stirs up five eggs with milk, salt and pepper. Then, seeing one egg left behind in the box, he feels sorry for it and stirs it in as well.

As the eggs begin to bond and thicken in the pan, Guy ponders his capacity to feel empathy for inanimate objects. On reflection, he decides that he doesn't, as a rule, care about non-living things. Only eggs. In fact, if he was given the choice between saving the life of a chicken or an egg, he'd save the egg. Not that a supermarket egg is alive, but still . . .

Lisa is suddenly at his shoulder, staring with him into the pan. 'What do you think?' she says, stepping back and spreading her arms in a tell-me-I-look-gorgeous-or-I'll-hit-you gesture.

'What's that top made out of? Sandpaper?'

'It's spangly.'

'Isn't it itchy?'

'It's cool.'

'It could be cool *and* itchy.'

'It's not itchy.'

'You're just saying that because you know it looks cool.'

'So you think it's cool?'

'I always said it was cool. I just think it also looks itchy.'

'Well it isn't.'

'You sure?'

'It isn't.'

4

'It *feels* itchy,' he says, squeezing her left tit.

'Well it isn't.'

And so on. A happy couple.

Although Lisa talked more, laughed more, drank more, fell over more, and generally lived more than Guy, she rarely went anywhere without him. They were so inseparable that it never occurred to anyone to wonder whether or not they were compatible. No one questioned the choice they had made to be together, since no choice seemed to have been involved. Guy'n'Lisa were a unit. They were an old and wonky armchair in the living room of their friends' social lives, so familiar and comfortable that it never occurred to anyone how worn-out it looked, or that it was never very tasteful in the first place.

Having finished their fillingless omelette, Lisa insists that Guy changes his clothes. She thrusts a few lurid T-shirts at him, which he tries on and promptly takes off, ending up in his original blue one, complete with an egg stain on the nipple and a belly dappled with washing-up water.

They bundle out of the house together and rush off to the party of a friend of a friend of Lisa's, with Guy already wondering what time they will be able to leave and hoping there are some decent magazines in the toilet.

2

The Horse and Cannon Pub in Holloway, possibly one of the earliest theme pubs in London, pretends to be a World War Two Anderson shelter crossed with a Thai restaurant. Inexplicable pieces of corrugated iron had been bolted on to the walls, with drinking booths formed by partitions made of bamboo.

Graham, with a highly developed taste for the inexplicable, considers this Satay–Spam theme to be a masterstroke of design, and despite living a brisk twenty-minute walk away, in a tiny flat just off the Caledonian Road, he only ever drinks with Guy at the Horse and Cannon, his aesthetic local.

A pager is lying between them, face up, in the puddle of beer which always forms in the centre of their favourite, warped table. Graham jabs it roughly with a finger, then picks it up, wipes it on his trousers, and holds it in the air.

'I'd only had it a few days,' he says. 'I mean, I was worried that I was missing phonecalls, and – you know – some auditions just happen at the last minute and you have to be ready to work at a moment's notice, and anyway, Zoe had been complaining that it was hard to get in touch with me, 'cause when I *am* working – which does happen occasionally, believe it or not – I could be anywhere, and it was pissing her off. So I got it, and for a while you don't get any messages or anything because no one has your number. But finally, it starts buzzing occasionally, and I'm – you know – happy.

'Then I'm walking down the road, on my way to an audition for some advert, and this thing buzzes in my pocket. It's only – like – the fourth message I've ever had, or something. And I stop walking, and press the Read button, and this message comes up: "DEAR G – HAVE FALLEN IN LOVE WI". I press it again, and it says, "TH SOMEONE ELSE – BEST NOT SPEA". Then I get, "K FOR A WHILE – HOPE WE CAN STIL" and "L BE FRIENDS – LOVE Z."'

Graham puts the pager back into the puddle of beer and stares at Guy, waiting for a reaction.

Guy's sympathy, after a long frown, extends to 'You're taking the piss!'

'I'm not.'

'Really?'

'Yeah.'

'She persuaded you to get a pager, waited a few days, then used it to chuck you?'

'Yeah.'

'After – what – two months?'

'Six.'

'*Six?*'

'Yeah.'

'Shit – that's awful.'

'I couldn't believe it. And – like – I still had to go to the audition. And it was for this drink that's supposed to make your smile glow like a monkey's arse or something. And I had to do all this happy, smiley stuff, then the casting director came up to me to have a look at my teeth, and the weirdest thing happened.'

'What?'

'I . . . like . . . I started crying.'

'In the middle of the audition?'

'Yeah. This woman touched me on the lips to get a better look at my teeth, and suddenly this wave of emotion hit me, and I just started blubbing.'

'What did she do? She chuck you out?'

'Course not. I was in tears.'

'So what did she do?'

'Well – she was a bit taken aback at first. Then she gave me this long hug and rubbed my back and told me it would all be OK and asked me what had happened and talked me through everything, and the whole thing was – like – an amazing experience. She made me see things about Zoe that I'd never understood before. It was like she was clairvoyant. She told me I was too good for her, and that anyone who chucks their boyfriend on a pager has a sadistic streak. She said I need more kindness and less aggression in my life. Within half an hour, she understood me better than Zoe did in six months. I mean, women like that have an incredible perspective on life. The way she talked to me was . . . just . . . there was something really horny about the whole experience.'

'Horny?'

'Yeah.'

'Being comforted while you cry over an ex-girlfriend is horny?'

'Not usually. I mean – you wouldn't expect it to be. But the way she did it was incredible.'

'Why? What did she do?'

'It wasn't what she did – it was how she did it.'

'How did she do it, then?'

'It wasn't – like – a technique or something. It's just the way she was.'

'What are you talking about?'

'You know. She's . . .'

'What? She's what?'

'She's . . . like . . . older.'

'Older than what?'

'Than us.'

'She's old? This is what you find so horny? That she's old?'

'Not really old. It's not a necrophilia thing. She's just . . . like . . . forty or something. Well preserved. She's mature. I tell you, she makes Zoe seem like a baby. In every way. I mean – people our age are . . . are just . . . there's nothing to us. All we've got going for us is the fact that we haven't yet gone wrinkly – and if you think about it for more than one second, you have to face the fact that a face without wrinkles has absolutely no character, and is therefore totally unsexy. Our faces are blank. They don't say anything. Only old people are beautiful.'

'So she's beautiful?'

'Yeah. Sort of. If you adjust your values to take account of ageing.'

'You fancy this woman? Is that what you're trying to tell me?'

'Yeah. In a spiritual kind of way.'

'Not a physical way?'

'The physical thing's not important any more. That's what I'm saying. The whole thing's given me a different perspective on life. I'm not interested in pushy, pert little bitches any more. That whole Zoe era is over. I want something more . . . you know . . . mature. Older women are . . . like . . . I mean . . . it's legal. And the possibilities are endless. It's completely uncharted water.'

'You don't think anyone's ever tried to shag middle-aged women before?'

'I'm not talking about all middle-aged women. Just this casting director. She's incredible.'

'Hm.'

'What d'you mean, *hm*?'

'Just – you know – hm.'

'Hm isn't a word. It doesn't mean anything.'

'It means plenty.'

'It means nothing.'

'It means I don't believe you. Which is why you're getting uptight.'

'Are you calling me a bullshitter?'

'Yes.'

'*Yes?*'

'You want to know what I think?' says Guy.

'Course I do.'

'About your big revelation.'

'*Yes.*'

'Zoe dumped you. You feel humiliated. So you latch on to the first person who gives you five minutes of attention, then come up with some hugely elaborate justification for what you're feeling, when you're not in fact feeling anything at all. Your brain, your dick and your emotions are all in suspended animation, and you're in the temporary state where it's impossible to have one single rational thought about women. You're on the rebound. Everyone goes through it, and it's completely normal, and the most important part of the whole process is that your friends come to the pub with you and pretend to take you seriously, when in fact you're going through those vital few weeks in which you'll only be capable of talking complete bollocks.'

Graham stares at Guy, blinking.

'So it's fine,' says Guy. 'Carry on. You know – talk about it more, if you want. That's what I'm here for.'

'Talk about what?'

'Anything. Tell me how you feel.'

'Fuck off!'

'Don't get aggressive.'

'You've . . . you're . . . you've ruined the whole thing, now.'

'What whole thing?'

'Just – if that's your idea of sympathy . . .'

'Course it's sympathy. I'm listening, aren't I?'

'Listening? Lecturing me for ten minutes on what an idiot I am is not listening. It's . . . it's . . . lecturing.'

'Graham – you've been barking on all evening about some wrinkly old woman who you're never even going to see again. *That* is called listening. And if you want to go on about her for the rest of the evening, that's fine. If it helps you pretend you're not upset about Zoe, that's cool. I just thought you might want to know that in two days' time you're not going to remember this woman even exists, and you're *certainly* never going to sleep with her.'

'For your information, I am going to see her again. It's already arranged.'

'Don't tell me you asked her out. You didn't ask her out.'

'No. She rang me. It was a mutual thing. We really clicked, Guy. She told me I was too good for the soft-drink advert, and I deserve better. Then she offered me an audition for this Ibsen thing – a theatre job – and told me she looked forward to seeing me there.'

'You going?'

'Course I am.'

'What if she makes a pass?'

'It's not like that. Something profound is going on between us. I told you. It's a new era of my life.'

'You've lost it.'

'I'm moving forward, Guy. It's very exciting.'

'You've definitely lost it.'

3

'What do you mean, *grateful*?' says Lisa.

'Just – grateful. You know. Grateful,' says Keri.

'But –. . .'

'Like I was doing him a favour.'

'What's wrong with that? It sounds nice.'

'It's not, Lisa. It's awful.'

'You can't chuck someone just because they're grateful.'

'Of course you can. How are you supposed to *stay* with someone who's grateful?'

'Easily. I'd love it. If Guy was grateful occasionally, it would be fantastic.'

'That's different. If you're with someone a long time they've got to make an effort. If you're just starting, it's the worst thing you can do.'

'*Why?*'

'If someone behaves like I'm doing him a favour by going out with him, I just . . . want to run away.'

Keri swishes the last dregs of coffee round her cup, swills it down, then swivels her chair away from the table to catch a feeble burst of sunlight. Were Lisa not her oldest friend, this would be a gesture of blank dismissal; instead it simply comes across as a spot of mid-sentence sunbathing.

Lisa looks at Keri's profile, angled up to catch the sun, and sighs. With her aquiline nose, flawless skin, funky smile, perfect size-ten figure, neck-revealingly cropped nut-brown hair, neat little tits and general air of *über*-species beauty, any man who got Keri into bed, it was clear, would naturally feel more than a little grateful.

'He was gorgeous, though,' says Lisa.

'He was all right.'

'And nice. He was a nice guy.'

'I told you. He was a pain in the arse.'

'You didn't say that. You just said he was grateful.'

'Same thing.'

'What's wrong with a bit of gratitude?'

'It wasn't a *bit* of gratitude, Lisa. It was constant. He was always thanking me. Always.'

'For what?'

'For everything.'

'Everything?'

'Just about.'

'Sex?' says Lisa, with a smirk.

'*Yes!* That was the worst. Every time, after we slept together, he'd thank me. *Every time*. It was . . . it's . . . just so rude. I'd be lying there, and you're beginning to get your orientation back, and before I'd even remembered who I was, this voice would rise up from the next pillow and start thanking me. Can you believe that?'

Lisa laughs, and allows a short silence to open up before saying, 'You'd forget who you were?'

'What?' says Keri, frowning.

Lisa lowers her voice. 'You'd forget who you were? During sex?'

'What are you on about?'

'You just said you forgot who you were during sex. That's amazing. Was he . . . like . . . really good?'

'You always forget who you are. That's the whole point.'

'Is it?'

'Yeah.'

'Really?'

'Course it is.'

'Oh.'

'Why?' says Keri. 'Don't you?'

'Er . . . I don't think so.'

'You sure?'

'If you walked in in the middle, and asked me what my name was, I'd definitely remember,' says Lisa.

Keri chuckles. 'Is that bad? Is that your definition of bad sex?'

'I don't know. You're the one that said it.'

'I didn't!'

'Would you remember, though?' says Lisa.

'What – if someone walked into my bedroom with a clipboard while I was having sex and asked me what my name was?'

'Yes,' replies Lisa, her face puckered with concern.

'Um . . . I think I probably would,' says Keri. 'I'd be surprised, but I'd remember my name.'

'Oh. Right.'

'You feel better now?'

'Don't patronize me.'

'I'm not! Lisa – this is the most ridiculous conversation. What are you so paranoid about?'

Lisa stares at Keri. They both know that with regard to Keri, Lisa's paranoias cover every aspect of human dignity. Lisa is less beautiful, less successful, has a less interesting sex life, and generally lives a dwarfish existence by comparison to her friend.

The only thing Lisa has over Keri is her relationship with Guy. For all Keri's attractions, she never seemed able – in fact never seemed to want to keep a boyfriend for longer than a few weeks. Every so often, Keri showed a flicker of jealousy for the stability in Lisa's life; the rest of the time Lisa felt more like a disciple than a friend.

'Shall we walk?' says Lisa, nodding in the vague direction of Primrose Hill.

'OK,' replies Keri.

'Or have another coffee?'

'OK.'

'Another coffee,' says Lisa, wrinkling her nose.

Keri nods, and with one eyebrow effortlessly summons the waiter.

*   *   *

'There's this guy at my office you should meet,' says Lisa, as they stand on top of the hill, gazing at the rippled halo of pollution hanging low over London.

Keri ignores her, annoyed and amazed at the speed with which Lisa could write off her ex-boyfriends and start trying to find a replacement.

'He's called Josh. You'll really like him. He's very cool.'

Keri ignores her more concertedly, turning to look in the opposite direction, at the restricted view to the north. Lisa's insistence that it was impossible to be single and happy at the same time was an unwelcome cornerstone of their friendship. Regardless of all opposition, the minute Keri became single Lisa would mount a series of forceful, grating attempts to set her up with men.

However much Keri resented this, she could never quite make her resistance fully clear. To insist that she was genuinely content on her own somehow felt embarrassing – as if it was an insult to Lisa, a challenge to her relationship with Guy.

Lisa's wilful refusal to acknowledge Keri's dislike of her romantic interference had, over time, worn down Keri's defences. Lisa used quiet coercion to push Keri into listening to detailed descriptions of her single male friends, and often invited her to crudely obvious matchmaking dinners using a tone which threatened that refusal would be taken badly. Compliance had somehow become a duty.

Lisa asserted herself over Keri with the skilful manipulation of guilt – making Keri feel that she was so loaded with good fortune that any snub was a last straw, a final insult from someone whose life was blessed, yet who wouldn't do the slightest thing to help a friend for whom everything was so much harder, so much less fair. Lisa behaved as if Keri's luck, her looks and her success constituted a moral debt to her old friend, who had year by year been increasingly outshone.

No matter how frequently and how far Keri moved to accommodate Lisa's wishes, she always remained one misdemeanour away from a telling-off. Equally, getting through to Lisa that Keri enjoyed being single was a genuine impossibility.

'He's actually very good-looking and he doesn't even realize it,' continues Lisa, before a scuffing of trainers on gravel prompts her to turn towards Keri, just in time to see her set off down the hill.

'Sorry,' says Lisa, trotting behind. 'You're probably not ready. It was just an idea.'

'Forget it.'

'Maybe in a while . . .'

'Maybe not,' says Keri, through a clenched jaw.

'We'll see,' replies Lisa, smiling to herself.

4

The offices of Elemental Productions consisted of a series of rooms, each about the size of an average family freezer, suspended from the rafters of a large block in Soho. Originally designed as residential accommodation for midgets with agoraphobia, the landlords had cleverly realized that due to the proliferation of television companies, all of which need to be in Soho and none of which ever succeeds in getting any programmes on screen, it was possible to make even more money from these impossibly small rooms by kicking out the midgets and bringing in the TV wannabes, has-beens and never-will-bes.

Elemental Productions was one of the most prosperous companies on their floor of the building. Having succeeded in getting a series of four half-hour programmes on Channel 4 at eleven-thirty on Tuesday nights during the February of 1996, the production fee (of £25,000) had been keeping the company afloat for the succeeding three years of development work.

This lack of resources made little dent in the calibre of the employees, however, and the office was staffed by rotating groups of fresh graduates from top universities working for no pay. The company was owned, administered and run by Geoff Beckton, who also produced every film. He only paid himself a salary when Elemental was in production, and as a result he hadn't bought himself any new clothes since . . . well, since February 1996. He also hadn't been in a good mood since that same month.

The one thing that cheered him up was his first task of the day: opening the stack of fifty CVs which arrived in the post every morning, browsing through the begging letters, then throwing all but a clutch into the bin, secure in the knowledge that the world was full of people even more unsuccessful than him.

The only CVs he kept were the ones from recent graduates with good degrees wanting to 'get their foot in the door'. Elemental Productions, like the whole industry, was entirely dependent on the free labour supplied by arts graduates in their early twenties suffering from the temporary delusion that having an interesting job was more important than earning enough money to pay rent.

Most people would realize after a couple of months that they were being exploited and would embark on a career crisis, possibly indulge in a nervous breakdown, then go home and beg their parents for enough money to get a genuine qualification in something along the lines of law, accountancy or business studies. If their parents refused, possibly on the grounds that seventeen years of education really ought to be enough to acquire at least one marketable skill, then these unfortunate ex-TV-wannabes would resort to management consultancy.

Meanwhile, a handful of people clung on in the industry out of sheer obstinacy, and if they were lucky began to earn what could almost be called a living wage as a researcher. Whenever there was nothing in production, however, the job title changed to development researcher and the salary went down.

The two development researchers' at Elemental Productions were Lisa and Josh. Alongside Geoff, they were the only permanent employees. (That is, if the word 'permanent' can be used to refer to a series of three-month contracts renewed on the Friday afternoon of the week they expired.)

Although Lisa had taken an instant dislike to Josh when he first arrived, she had grown to like him, and their relationship had slowly developed to a pitch of exuberant flirtatiousness. Lisa took a positively indecent interest in Josh's complex love life, and the first couple of hours of each day would generally be spent on the exchange of saucy secrets and intimate details. This exchange, however, was almost entirely one way. Josh would spill a few stories about his latest encounters, gently modifying his repeated failures into modest successes, followed by Lisa telling a story from her life which somehow revealed precisely nothing about her relationship with Guy.

Josh came to hate the word 'we' more than any other in the English language. Often Josh's eyes would glaze over as Lisa was relating an account of her weekend, his mind losing itself in tallying the number of times she used the word 'I' against 'we'. 'We' always won.

Lisa never talked about anything Guy had done wrong, or described any arguments, or even criticized him. Other than the effect he had on Lisa's personal pronouns, Guy barely made an entrance in her stories at all. Despite frequent, sweaty surges of curiosity, Josh never dared probe into their relationship, and as a result had only a hazy notion of Guy as an odd mixture of the perfect male, and Satan.

Even though he'd never met him, Josh hated Guy. He wanted him dead.

Aside from these occasional homicidal urges, Josh kept only one secret from Lisa. A rather fundamental secret. In fact, a secret which had major repercussions on almost every conversation they ever had.

His fascinating sex life, when it came down to it, didn't exist. The entire thing was made up in order to impress her.

Although each individual story was only slightly changed, the cumulative picture he had given her – of a haphazardly raunchy canter through the bedrooms of London – somehow bore no relation to the truth. The fact was, Josh never closed the deal. Despite his unceasing efforts, an endless series of almosts, nearlys and not-quites rarely got him any more than the kind of gratification an adolescent would expect of an average Saturday night.

There was no particular reason for Josh's lack of a sex life. He was tall, good-looking, and although he only earned £200 a week, he had the kind of job that came across well at parties. To look at him, you'd never imagine quite how little sex he had performed in his life. Not only could he count his total number of partners on a minority of his fingers, he could count the actual number of *times* he had shagged without any genuine headway into double figures.

The closest Josh ever came to an explanation for this phenomenon was that it had become self-perpetuating. As soon as he found himself speaking to any woman who used even the vaguest allusion to a hint of a suggestion of sexual availability, he found himself giving off an air of desperation that operated like a sudden attack of poisonous body odour. Women simply walked away from him.

The problem had started during adolescence, when, through a series of unfortunate coincidences, he had somehow taken an unfeasibly long time to lose his virginity. Despite the fact that there was nothing *wrong* with him, he had managed to turn twenty-one before ever having sex. As a result, when his desperation odour didn't have its usual effect and he found himself in bed with a woman, even *during sex* he found himself wrestling with the notion that he was repulsive to women. Nothing, it seemed, could compensate for the indignity of having been such a failure for so long.

Each time he found himself getting somewhere with a new partner he'd try to convince himself that this would lay to rest his paranoia, but he'd always emerge feeling that he had to have sex with just one more person, and she had to be just a little better looking than the one before. Only then would he feel genuinely self-confident, and would his sexual body odour begin to clear up.

Josh knew it was childish and depressingly English to blame all your neuroses on school, but he couldn't escape the idea that he was still recovering from his single-sex education. Brought up with two brothers and no sisters, then sent to a school entirely without girls, Josh had never quite grown out of the lingering suspicion that females were in fact aliens.

Even at university, Josh had managed to hide away in the relative safety of the sporty male-dominated clique who ruled his student-union bar. This crowd wasn't exclusively masculine, but the interlopers did tend to be the kind of girls who wore rugby tops and had lots of brothers.

It was with this selection of women that his group of friends – the loudest and cockiest boys in the university – all lost their virginity. While this had been a useful enough experience, Josh hadn't found it particularly pleasurable, and had never quite got over his revulsion at the fact that these girls all had bendy fingers from playing too much hockey. The only aspect of his clique's virginity-loss to give him any real pleasure was that following their sexual initiation, his friends' predilection for taking their dicks out in public began to wane, which came as an immense relief to Josh, who had never found the whole exercise particularly dignified in the first place.

Lisa, who Josh had known for six months, was his first proper female friend. Never before had Josh felt relaxed enough with a woman to feel he had enough leeway to show his true personality. He regretted now that he had let himself get sucked into a cycle of lies, but having started, it seemed impossible to stop. Even so, although the content of much of what he said contained barely a fragment of truth, the way he was saying it somehow made Josh feel that he was communicating exactly who he was. For the first time, he was allowing a woman to see what he was really like.

Josh's usual lack of self-confidence vanished when he was in Lisa's company. Given that his university friends were, in the cold light of day, an immensely dislikeable collection of individuals, and the only two people he had kept in touch with from school were now in America and psychiatric care respectively, Lisa was perhaps Josh's only real friend.

Real friend, that is, leaving aside the minor complication of his explosive, near-perpetual urge to rip her clothes off and roger her senseless on the office floor.

5

What Lisa liked best about Josh was his desperation to please her. He was the one man she knew who was open about his need to be liked. His insecurities with women were so obvious and so inexpertly buried that Lisa felt her liking for him came with a moral duty. Of all the women in his life, only she had made the effort to see through the veneer of fabrication and bullshit to the inner man, who just needed a little help to be himself. And Lisa knew she could do this for him. She could cure him.

If Josh could just get somewhere with a sexy woman, his self-confidence would return, he'd stop coming across as over-keen and he would begin to have the success he deserved. He didn't need a relationship – he wasn't ready for that – he just needed a quick fling with someone who looked good on his arm and made him feel like he'd achieved something. He was a genuinely attractive guy, after all, but until he'd had the attention of a comparable woman, he'd never realize it. The answer was clear. Keri and Josh were made for one another. Lisa decided to stage a matchmaking meal which, she felt sure, couldn't fail.

Guy thought this was a disastrous idea. He didn't

like dinner parties anyway, and the combination of people sounded awful. He was always pleased to have Keri over for some food, but Lisa's constant attempts to set her up with men always struck Guy as tacky and embarrassing. Josh, in particular, sounded like a no-hoper. Although Guy had never met him, something in the naggingly flattering way Lisa always described Josh had given Guy the firm impression that he was a dick. The more Lisa protested that Guy would like him, the more Guy secretly decided he was going to hate Josh's guts.

*   *   *

'What are you doing?' says Lisa, walking into the kitchen to find Guy weighing a knob of butter.

'What's it look like?'

'You don't need to weigh butter.'

'Why? Does it weigh itself?'

'It's just butter. Shove in a lump. It doesn't make any difference.'

Guy, who tends to cook in the style of a twelve-year-old doing his first chemistry experiment, ignores her. Winking to eliminate parallax error on the scales, he scoops a corner off his piece of butter to get precisely fifty grams. Tipping the butter into the pan, Guy catches her eye. 'What?' he says, mock-innocently.

She smiles at him, shaking her head.

Guy points a finger at the recipe book, and says, 'Can you pass me ten grams of basil?'

Lisa, emitting a growl of exasperation, steps towards him and kisses him full on the mouth.

'Mnmnm gmmmnnm mgngmmnn,' he says.

Lisa stops kissing him, and licks her lips. 'What?'

'Snogging isn't in the recipe, you know.'

'Why are you such a dick?' she says, staring into his eyes.

He shrugs. 'I guess I'm just lucky.'

'You're going to like Josh,' she says.

'I'm sure I am.'

'You are. Really.'

'I know.'

'He's nice.'

'Of course he is,' says Guy, feeling a renewed sense of dread at the awfulness of the man who is about to enter his house.

*   *   *

The dinner party, in the end, was a relative success thanks to the conversation-inducing powers of alcohol.

Guy's pre-prepared hatred of Josh was confirmed within seconds of his arrival, Guy instantly clocking him as a sexually repressed public schoolboy with an anal fixation, a latent violent streak and a crippling inability to relax in the presence of women. Josh, meanwhile, was relieved to register Guy as a boring, badly dressed git with a jealous temperament who wasn't even good-looking and didn't remotely deserve Lisa.

The barely disguised hostility Josh was receiving from Guy combined with the presence of the staggeringly gorgeous Keri would usually have rendered Josh speechless with nerves. Fortunately, however, the conversation split into two, and he only had to converse with Lisa for the crucial not-yet-drunk stage of the meal. It was slightly worrying that Keri was so patently ignoring him, abetted by Guy, but at least it made the evening less stressful.

Keri, having glanced at him on the way in, felt entirely indifferent to Josh. She turned her back and spent the entire meal talking to Guy. Although Guy teetered on the brink of dullness, she had always liked him, and there was something kind in his eyes and in his smile which she found mysteriously sexy. Although they'd never really had any profound conversations, and had never spent any time alone together, an odd unspoken intimacy hung in the air between them as the two people who really knew Lisa – who saw how much of herself she chose to hide – who understood the subtle aggression behind her social façade. Keri admired Guy for putting up with Lisa for so long. In her disloyal moments, she even wondered why he bothered.

With Guy burbling on about some American sitcom, Keri's eyes drifted across the table to Lisa and Josh, engrossed in an intense conversation. Suddenly, out of the blue, Keri understood why Lisa interfered so enthusiastically in her sex life. Lisa was trapped.

She was obsessed with Keri's single status not because she thought it made Keri unhappy, but out of envy. Lisa wasn't taking pity on Keri – she was jealous of her freedom.

Lisa, Keri realized, didn't want her cosy, supportive relationship. She couldn't admit it, but she wanted what Keri had. She wanted random and disastrous sex with a series of fickle, selfish bastards, not a loving, considerate boyfriend.

Guy wasn't consciously possessive or clinging – he was just stable and loyal – which, basically, was pretty boring. Lisa, in her comfortable flat with her comfortable boyfriend and her comfortable job, was bored. Keri was living the life of a young person; Lisa, out of inertia, was missing out.

With a stab of outrage, it dawned on Keri that as Lisa's boredom had grown, she had begun using Keri as a means of vicariously sleeping with men she fancied.

Keri's refusal to acknowledge Josh had two beneficial effects. Firstly, it gave him two hours' adjustment time to her presence, which was the minimum required for Josh to stand a chance of sustaining a conversation without emitting his desperation odour. Secondly, by the time Keri finally did take a proper look at him, she was already deeply pissed, the effect of which was that she found him instantly sexy – sexy enough to override the confusing swirl of resentment towards

Lisa which was sloshing heavily around her head. He had good arms, strong-looking hands and an OK face. Best of all, he didn't talk too much.

The alcohol in her bloodstream had by now given Keri the horn, and her first proper look at Josh was a big, open smile with generous blow-job lips. He'd do. He'd scratch the itch.

Lisa, who had spent most of the evening dropping leaden hints to Guy that the pair of them ought to leave the room, was almost giving up hope of Keri and Josh even exchanging words. She was increasingly annoyed with Keri for ignoring Josh, annoyed with Guy for ignoring her hints, and annoyed with Josh for seeming happy to talk to her all evening. Then the phone rang, Guy disappeared to answer it, Lisa made a dive for the kitchen, and when she returned a few minutes later, the pair of them were flirting like tango dancers.

Guy comes back from the phone looking sombre.

'It's Helen,' he says. 'She's been stood up.'

'What? Again?' says Lisa.

Guy nods. 'She's only down the road. She's coming round.'

'Oh, *Guy*!'

'What?'

'She's so . . .'

'What?'

'She's so depressing. We're supposed to be having a dinner party.'

'There's loads left. She can have some.'

Lisa rolls her eyes and catches Josh's eye. 'You've got to meet this girl. Guy snogged her ten years ago on some holiday and he's been in love with her ever since.'

'BOLLOCKS!'

'It's true,' continues Lisa. 'Guy's a victim fetishist. What he loves about Helen is that she's always miserable. Whenever you meet her, you can guarantee that something awful will have just happened to her, and she'll be really unhappy about it all, and the whole thing just gives Guy the biggest hard-on you've ever seen.'

'FUCK OFF!'

'I tell you – she's so boring that when Guy's arranged to meet her, I never go, because I'm genuinely afraid that I'll fall asleep in her company. Either that, or I'd find myself slapping her around the face and telling her to cheer up and sort her life out. She really is *so bleak*. Then – and this is guaranteed – after he's seen her, Guy will come back, tell me Helen's latest sob story, and almost immediately, he'll try and shag me.'

'RUBBISH!'

'It's true. Honestly. I don't mind. It's just funny, that's all, 'cause it's the story of Helen's life. It really is. She makes men want to fuck someone else. She does. It's her gift.'

'Don't be such a bitch. Helen's a great person.'

34

' "A great person?" When Guy starts describing you as "a great person", it's time to kill yourself. It means you're a social dalek.'

Guy, who spent most of his life confident that he'd end up marrying Lisa, felt a surge of hatred. How could he possibly love someone who was so callous? Lisa's occasional attacks on Helen, which always seemed to happen in public, always hit a raw nerve with Guy. He felt fiercely protective towards Helen – who had been exploited, scorned and rejected by so many people – and seethed at the sight of his own girlfriend joining the mob.

Not wanting a confrontation in front of Lisa's friends, Guy gives a thin smile and ducks into the kitchen. He fills the sink and begins washing up – his private signal to Lisa that he is pissed off.

When the doorbell goes, Guy swiftly dries his hands and marches to the entry-phone without even glancing at the three bodies in his living room. After a swift mutter he buzzes Helen in, then rushes to the door of the flat to greet her.

Helen's arrival has precisely the effect Lisa had predicted. Almost immediately, her unhappiness filters out into the room and overcomes both Josh and Keri with the sudden urge to have sex with someone other than Helen. They need to get away from her, to get away from her shroud of depression, to do something life-affirming – to fuck.

With just a moment's eye contact, this desire passes

between them. They stand up in unison, smirking. Lisa offers to ring for a cab, but they turn her down, insisting that they're tired and will be able to hail a taxi in the street. They simply have to get out of there as quickly as possible, and into bed.

Within a minute they are on the pavement, waving at passing cabs, laughing together in the fresh, cool Helen-free air.

Lisa watches them from a top-floor window, amazed that her plan has worked, surprised at the speed with which it all happened, and in the back of her mind, unsettlingly miserable at the sight of Josh with his arm around another woman.

Guy, meanwhile, is comforting Helen after yet another slight at the hands of some man who has let her down, supposedly without provocation. Not wanting to suffer Helen's moaning, Lisa watches Josh and Keri drive away, then turns to the sink and carries on with Guy's unfinished washing-up.

Sitting next to Guy on the sofa, Helen tries to tell him about her awful evening, but she feels inhibited by the splashing and plate-clattering coming through the doorway from the kitchen. Even from an adjacent room, Lisa manages to intimidate her.

Dim enough to aspire to cleverness without knowing what it was or that she didn't possess any, plump, and with the conversational charms of a snowplough, Lisa was the one person in the world Helen truly detested. As a human being, she was a waste of space. Her existence was a waste of oxygen, a waste of food and a waste of time for everyone who had to listen to her talk. She didn't deserve five minutes of Guy's life, let alone the full half-share which she so enthusiastically gobbled up.

Still, if Helen wanted to see Guy, she had to see Lisa, and at least this was an opportunity to talk to him without Lisa's piggy eyes glaring accusingly at her.

Guy smiles at Helen, his head cocked sympathetically on one side. Her precise words are rather passing him by as he gazes at her, lost in contemplation of her eyes. She has the most fathomless, brown-black eyes of anyone he knows, each pupil merging invisibly into the darkness of her iris, always moist, as if on the brink of tears.

Few people saw Helen as beautiful, but for Guy she represented a certain kind of murky perfection. The light-sucking thick black curls of her hair, the molten-tar smudges of her eyes and the subtly downcast curve of her mouth somehow conveyed a truth about the sadness of the world. She had the most honest face he had ever seen.

There was something in Helen's unhappiness that Guy admired. It was somehow more real than anything his other friends chose to fill their lives with. She was confronting what she took most seriously.

While everyone else used their spare time schizo-phrenically – leaping from half-bored laziness to sudden, frenetic bouts of fun-seeking – Helen, calmly and single-mindedly, was suffering. She was the only one of Guy's friends who seemed to know what she wanted – misery – and to live a focused and settled life pursuing it.

Her constant unhappiness was, in some way, an accusing finger pointing out the futility in everyone else's lives. When Guy was in the company of Helen, depression somehow seemed a more impressive state of mind than happiness. With her, he stopped wanting to be happy. Happiness seemed superficial. He wanted to be in touch with what really mattered in life. He wanted to be like her. He wanted to be depressed.

The pair of them talk until two in the morning, by which time Helen has marginally cheered up. Guy kisses her goodbye, brushes his teeth as fast as he can, and hops noisily into bed.

Lisa remains fast asleep.

He rolls her on to her back, but still she doesn't flicker an eyelid.

Guy turns to face the wall and gives his penis a friendly squeeze. Almost instantly, he has a fistful of thirsty, swollen cock.

Maybe Lisa did have a point about Helen's effect on people.

6

Josh was late for work the next day. Lisa tried to make a few phonecalls and concentrate on her work, but she was too distracted by her excitement at what might have happened the previous night between her best friend and her colleague.

When Josh finally entered the office, she only had to see the bounce in his walk to know that he had shagged Keri.

He smiles, clocking Lisa's reaction to his arrival. 'Tea?' he chirps.

Lisa grins, with a hint of lasciviousness. She scrutinizes his face for a while, then says, 'Please.'

'EG or PG?'

'EG. Weak.'

'Weak it is,' says Josh, spinning from the room and skipping downstairs to the kettle.

Lisa listens to the distant growl of the boiling kettle, and shuffles a few papers around on her desk. In the back of her head, a tiny voice squeaks at her: *You have a problem. A certain level of curiosity about your friends' sex lives is only natural, but you have a problem.*

Piss off, she replies to herself, just as Josh returns carrying two cups of Earl Grey tea.

'One weak,' he says, placing a mug on Lisa's desk, 'one strong.'

He somehow manages to load the description of his own tea with overtones of virility, as he plants the cup in the middle of his desk and leans back in his chair, avoiding Lisa's gaze.

'Well?' she says.

'What?' he replies, trying not to smile.

They stare at one another across their shared desk, in mounting silence.

'Aren't you going to tell me what happened?' she says, eventually.

'Can't you guess?' he replies.

'She shagged you.'

'I shagged her.'

'And?'

'And what?'

'How was it?'

'How was it?'

'Yes.'

'*How was it?*'

'*Yes!*'

'Fan – tastic.'

'Really?' Lisa sips her tea, in an attempt to regain control of her mouth muscles, which seem to have formed themselves into a fixed grimace.

'Really. Me and her – we're just . . .'

'What?'

'I think we're – you know – very compatible.'

'What – sexwise?'

'Everythingwise.'

'Josh – please. You got pissed and slept together. I'm very pleased and everything, but I don't think you're quite in marriage territory yet.'

'Yet.'

'Oh, stop it.'

'I'm serious. If this thing keeps going – and I don't see any reason why it won't – we're . . . I mean . . . it's just perfect. We're perfect for each other.'

'Josh! Get a grip! You had a pissed shag. You've had plenty of pissed shags. They never lead anywhere.'

'I know I have. Of course I have. I'm not saying I haven't. I just mean . . . this one felt . . .'

Josh tailed away, feeling incapable of describing the significance of the experience he had shared with Keri. In fact, he didn't even want to tell Lisa just how profound his feelings for Keri had already become. This wasn't because their sex had, in physical terms, been that great. Strictly speaking, he'd been concentrating too hard on trying to give her pleasure for him to pay too much attention to his own enjoyment.

With Keri, Josh had found something far more profound than mere gratification. She represented a major breakthrough. She was by far the sexiest woman he had ever slept with. By any standards, she was a *sexy woman*. As a result, Josh finally felt that he had arrived. He had made it as a man. An unequivocally beautiful woman had given up her body to him, and he had pleasured her like a true professional. Well, not like a *professional* – there was nothing sordid about it – rather, he had thrilled her like an expert. A sexual expert.

It dawned on him that he had spent his entire adult life in the tail end of a protracted adolescence. His insecurities about unattractiveness, physical awkwardness and sexual incompetence were typical teenage problems that he had somehow never grown out of. But now, at a stroke, they'd been banished for good. Never again would he come across as desperate. His agonies were over. He was at last a fully initiated man, qualified to swing cocks with the best of them. From now on, when public nudity was called for, anxiety would no longer subtract those critical couple of centimetres from his manhood. Oh, no. Just the briefest memory of Keri would make him swell with pride.

'. . . Look,' he says, realizing that he's still in the middle of a sentence, 'the whole thing felt . . . just . . . unique. It was a completely different experience from all the other women I've . . . you know . . . been with. There was nothing casual about it. Honestly. It was like we weren't just having sex. It felt like we were actually –. . .'

'DON'T SAY IT!'

'What?'

'Don't say it.'

'Don't say what?'

'Don't tell me you were making love, or I'll puke all over your desk.'

'But we were.'

'That's it!'

'What?'

'I'm phoning her.'

'Don't!'

'I am.'

'Don't!'

'I'm going to have lunch with her.'

'Don't!'

'Piss off.'

Lisa picks up the phone, grinning broadly, flicks to the back of her diary, and dials Keri's work number.

'Hello?'

'Keri?' says Lisa. 'It's me.'

'Aaaaaaaaaaaaaaaaaaaaaaaahhh!'

'What?'

'Aaaaaaaaaaaaaaaaaaaaaaaaahhhh! Ohmygod. Is he there?'

'Err – yes.'

'Aaaaaaaaaaaaaaaaaaaaahhhhhhh! Oh nooooooo-oooo!'

'What?'

'Oh nooooooo! I fucked uuuuup! So baaaaadly.'

'Look. Let's have lunch.'

'Yes. Yes. Emergency lunch.'

'Where?'

'I don't knoooooooow. Oh my god. He's *in the room*!'

'Look – let's meet at that place.'

'Which place?'

'The place next door to the other one that's really crap.'

'Oh, right. OK. See you at one.'

'OK. Bit after. Bye.'

'Bye.'

Lisa hangs up and looks at Josh, who is suddenly crumpled up in his chair – deflated by a surge of fear.

'What did she say?' he snaps.

'We're having lunch.'

'But what did she *say*?'

'Nothing. She just . . . screamed a lot.'

'Oh, right,' says Josh, in an and-I-know-what-*that*-sounds-like tone of voice.

Lisa looks at him.

'What kind of screaming?' says Josh, suddenly. 'Good screaming or bad screaming?'

'Couldn't tell. Just screaming screaming.'

Lisa arrives at their regular sandwich bar near Holborn station – roughly half way between Soho and Keri's office in the City – to find Keri staring blankly into space. Sensing Lisa's arrival, Keri looks up and opens her mouth. Inhibited by the public surroundings, Keri mimes a silent scream.

Lisa rushes to the table and sits down. 'Well?' she says.

'I'm such an *idiot*! I can't believe I . . . Oh, god . . . Oh godohgod . . . What a dis*a*ster!'

'Why?'

'I'm just . . . such a . . . I mean, I don't even like him. I don't like him. Not remotely. He's a dick. I . . . whenever I get drunk I just . . . What a nightmare!'

'Why? What went wrong?'

'What went *wrong*?'

'Yes,' says Lisa, puzzled.

'He's a . . . he's a . . .' Feeling her voice rise with indignation, Keri pauses and takes a breath. Something anxious in Lisa's expression inhibits her from giving vent to her full loathing of Josh. 'Look,' she continues. 'He's your friend. What happened isn't important. It just didn't work.'

Lisa's eyes widen with curiosity. 'Tell me.'

'There's nothing to tell. We just don't like each other.'

'Tell me.'

'Lisa . . .'

'*Tell me*. He's bad in bed?'

'It's not just that.'

'He is bad?'

Keri nods. 'Among other things, yes.'

'How bad?'

'Lisa . . .'

'How bad?'

'I thought he was your friend!' says Keri.

'He is. Tell me how bad.'

Keri stares at Lisa, not speaking. 'Just . . . you know,' she replies, after a loaded silence.

'I *don't* know.'

'Clumsy.'

'Clumsy?'

'And over-keen.'

'Right,' says Lisa, frowning. 'OK.'

'The whole thing was terrible. Believe me. You haven't been single for years, Lisa. I can't explain to you just how *bad* it can be. Really.'

'I've – . . .'

'You haven't. You have never had a shag quite as unpleasant as the . . . the . . . Oh god.'

'Look – I haven't even got a sandwich yet. Will you tell me?'

'I *have* told you.'

'Tell me properly what happened. Please.'

'Why?'

'Please.'

Keri nods and sighs. 'You've got a filthy mind.'

Lisa leaps up, grabs the first baguette that comes to hand and sits back down at the table, tearing at the stretchy bread with her teeth.

'Well?'

Keri looks up, slowly. 'He's one of those . . .'

'What?'

Keri leans in, and lowers her voice to a whisper. 'He's one of those people who's in such a rush that they actually try and . . . you know . . . shove it up . . . before either of you – not just me – but before *either* of us is ready. You know what I mean?'

'What? He's not even . . . hard?'

'Sort of . . . semi-hard. Frankfurter-hard. And he tries to push it up, and of course it won't go, so he gives up, you untangle your legs, he snogs you a bit more, mauls you with his fingers, and after a while he tries again, but he still isn't ready, so he goes back to kissing you and groping you, and you go through the whole process a few times, by which stage you're totally fed up with the whole thing, but eventually he massages himself towards enough of a stiffy to somehow ram it up, and it's like a cucumber in a sandpit, and the whole thing actually hurts, and you've given up on the whole idea of even remotely enjoying it ages ago, and you're just waiting for him to finish, but he goes *on* and *on* and *on*, thinking he's being really unselfish and is a great lover because he's not going to let himself come until you've come, so eventually you realize that the only way you can end the whole thing is to fake an orgasm, and you end up actually issuing orders and shouting in his ear, "Yes! Come! Come inside me!" and you're only doing it as a last desperate fucking attempt to get him to leave you alone, which *eventually* he does, then he insists on cuddling you because he thinks *that* makes him a good lover, and after a while you say, "Go to sleep. You were amazing," because that's the only way to get him off you, and you know that's all he wants to do anyway, so finally he rolls away and falls asleep, and you get up, go to the kitchen, have a slice of toast, and get into the shower.'

Lisa, still only one mouthful into her baguette, swallows. She takes another bite and chews slowly, the pair of them sitting in silence.

'Right,' she says, eventually.

'You happy now?' says Keri.

'What does that mean?' snaps Lisa, defensively.

'Now I've slept with him for you?'

Keri watches Lisa's mind spin as she thinks of how to react. Her eyes narrow slightly, and just as Keri expects, she goes on the attack.

'Don't try and blame me, Keri. I just gave you both a meal. If you insist on shagging him even though you don't like him then that's your problem. Don't act like you did it as a favour to me.'

'Is that what I said? Did I say it was a favour?'

'You just – as usual – try and blame someone else for your mistakes.'

'OK, Lisa. It was my fault. I know that. But I don't want you setting me up with blokes any more, and if you give Josh my phone number I'll kill you.'

'Fine,' says Lisa.

'Fine.'

They stare at one another across the table.

'And he's got bad breath,' says Keri.

'He doesn't have bad breath.'

'He does.'

'He doesn't.'

'And he farts in his sleep.'

'No!'

'Yes. In his sleep.'

'Farts?'

'Quiet little seepy ones.'

'OK. That *is* bad. Maybe I won't give him your number.'

'Good.'

'Fine.'

'Fine.'

*   *   *

Josh hears Lisa climbing the stairs to their office, and hurriedly pretends to be engaged in some absorbing work. Since his computer isn't switched on and he can't locate a pen, this isn't very convincing.

'All right?' he says, as Lisa sweeps in.

'Yeah.'

She smiles at him, affectionately. Josh immediately detects a hint of sympathy in her bearing, and panics. 'What did she say?'

'Nothing.'

'You talked about it?'

'Sort of. Not really. Just chatted.'

'And?'

'Look, Josh – it's none of my business what happens between you two. I don't want to get involved and I'm not even that interested anyway. You'll just have to leave me out of it.'

'OK. Good idea. If we're going to . . . you know . . . it's not fair for you to be a go-between. You're right. I'll just give her a ring this evening.'

'Good idea.'

They both start on their afternoon's work for a few minutes, before Josh speaks again. 'Shall I ring her now?'

'This evening, I reckon.'

'OK. You're right,' he says. 'You're right. This evening. I'll do it. What's her number?'

'Sorry?'

'What's her number?'

'Her number?'

'Her phone number.'

'Her phone number?'

'Yeah,' he says. 'What is it? I forgot to ask.'

'You forgot?'

'Yeah. I was too excited.'

'Oh.'

'What is it?'

'Her phone number?'

'Yeah.'

'Her number?'

'Yeah.'

'The number of her phone?'

'Yeah.'

'At her house?'

Josh stares at her, not answering, his brow tensing into a frown.

'The number . . . of her phone . . . is . . . different. It's changed. She's changed numbers. She's just moved house. And the number I've got isn't her number any more.'

Josh, who had already copied Keri's number out of Lisa's diary during the lunch break and was simply asking in order to have a decent answer in case Keri asked him how he got her number when he phoned her, suddenly wanted to kill himself. Lisa was an appalling liar. Her evasion was painfully transparent. During their lunch date, Keri must have told Lisa not to give Josh her number. It was suddenly clear that Keri wasn't interested in him.

Watching Josh visibly age before her eyes, Lisa felt a rising urge to hug him. Keri was a bitch. She damaged people. Every man who ever entered her bed emerged a wreck. She had even forced Lisa into the awful position of being the one who broke the bad news to Josh, while Keri, as usual, swanned away unharmed from the emotional carnage she had caused.

It was so unfair. Poor Josh really deserved better. The whole idea of allowing Keri to toy with him had been unforgivably stupid. Keri had behaved predictably. She always did what she wanted and never worried about the consequences, since for her there never were any consequences. She had no conception of the pain she caused, and no desire to learn. In her parallel universe of the beautiful, people didn't scar. Keri always came out unscathed, and she never looked back. Lisa had been an idiot. She had handed a puppy to a vivisectionist.

While Josh stared into space, his body frozen, Lisa resisted the impulse to comfort him. He probably wanted to be alone. It wasn't fair on him to have a witness to his humiliation.

Lisa picks up a few papers and shuffles to the door. 'I've got some work to do downstairs,' she says.

Josh doesn't look up, or react. Swamped by guilt and anger, Lisa leaves.

Josh gazed at the wall, his mind pounding over what he could have done wrong. How had he offended her? Maybe he had been too cold towards her in the morning. Maybe he came across badly because he didn't show her how much he cared. Their night together had been so good that he must have done something awful in the morning to antagonize her. The only conceivable answer was that he had played it too cool.

What an idiot! He'd fucked the whole thing up by being a typical repressed male, utterly blind to the emotion sex always stirs up in women. After the precious secrets that had passed between them in bed, Josh had simply woken up the next day and acted towards her as if his life hadn't even changed. She had given herself up to him entirely, more than any other woman in his life, and he had trampled all over her by failing to acknowledge her sacrifice.

Josh suddenly understood his mistake, and saw what he had do to make amends. He wasn't going to involve Lisa. She was right to have stepped back. Keri had obviously told her that she was upset, and that she didn't want to get hurt any more. It was up to Josh to make up for his coldness.

Even though he had Keri's phone number, he now had no excuse for having it, so calling her wasn't an option. Keri might blame Lisa for helping Josh to contact her, and it would emerge that Lisa hadn't given him the number, then Lisa would challenge him, and she'd figure out that he'd nicked it from her diary, then *she'd* be pissed off, and things would get even worse.

No. He wasn't going to phone. After all, he didn't need to. He knew where she lived. He'd spent the night at her flat. After work, he'd go straight to her house and wait for her. He'd physically camp out on her doorstep until she turned up, then he'd tell her how sorry he was and how much he loved her. He'd convince her that she had nothing more to worry about. He'd throw himself at her feet; he'd give her a bunch of roses; he'd beg for her forgiveness with such conviction that she'd be forced to invite him back into her flat where they'd instantly fall to the floor in the hallway and make love even more passionately than they had before.

On second thoughts, he'd go home first, wash his penis, change his underwear, then go to Keri's flat.

7

Walking home in the minor daze that stems from a full day at work after a night with only a quarter-strip of mattress to sleep on, Keri is already half-way through her own front garden before she spots Josh, blocking the path to her front door, standing open-mouthed with a fistful of roses drooping from one hand and misery plastered across his features.

Keri feels the muscles in her legs weaken. Just the sight of him almost makes her crumple to the ground and enter respiratory failure. She has developed a major allergy to his presence.

'Keri!' he says, dropping his roses into a puddle and grabbing her hands. Due to her briefcase, this involves twisting her wrist at a painful angle and wedges a sharp corner of leather into her tit. 'I've been such an idiot,' he says. 'I've treated you so badly. I never want to hurt you again, Keri. I really don't. I promise you that our night together meant as much to me as anything else I've ever done.'

Keri stares at him, blankly. 'Errr . . . will you let go of my briefcase?' she says.

'Sorry.'

'That's OK.'

'Keri – I'll never treat you in such an offhand way

ever again. We can be happy together. I know we can. Please. Give me another chance.'

There is a long silence, which grows increasingly intense as Josh begins to blink faster and faster, his breathing becoming heavy and irregular.

Oh Christ, thinks Keri. He's going to cry.

'I'm not very good at dealing with situations like this,' says Keri, eventually.

Josh nods, his head bobbing an absurd amount, with the exaggerated movements of someone who is on the verge of utterly losing control.

'Could you step back a second?' says Keri. 'You're blocking the way.'

Josh edges off the path.

Keri smiles at him, shuffles forward, unlocks her front door, opens it, steps inside, and closes it behind her.

All of a sudden, Josh is alone, standing in a muddy patch of weeds, staring at her door.

In that position, he loses all track of time, and it is dark before he remembers who he is, where he lives, and how to get home.

Before he turns away, he pokes the stems of the roses through her door, where they hold firm in the stiff springs of the letter-box. He stares at the roses for a moment, flinching as they abruptly disappear, yanked through from the inside, becoming stripped clean in the process.

A cascade of petals drifts to the ground.

Inside, Keri carries her six thorny stalks to the kitchen and spears them into the bin.

8

Graham swears viciously as he discovers that the puddle in the middle of the table has soaked into the elbow of his shirt. Guy stares at him, perturbed by his friend's over-reaction. Every single evening spent at the Horse and Cannon ends, inevitably, with wet elbows. It's part of the pub's appeal.

'Are you sure you're all right?' says Guy.

'No I'm not fucking all right,' Graham snaps. 'My elbows are completely fucking soaked, aren't they?'

'I meant apart from that.'

'Apart from what?'

'How's the rest of you? As in, not your elbows.'

'Well – dry, I suppose.'

'Other than being dry.'

'Look,' says Graham, 'in general, I'm pissed off. Everything's turned to shit. OK? Is that what you want to know?'

'Why's everything so shit? You missing Zoe?'

'*Zoe?* It's not Zoe. I told you – I hate her. That whole thing was doomed anyway. The Zoe situation's fine. It's the other one.'

'What other one?'

Graham sighs and takes a deep slurp of beer. 'The casting director,' he mumbles.

'The old one? Are you serious?'

Graham nods sorrowfully.

'You haven't . . .'

'No, no, no. The whole thing's just got a bit out of control.'

'How?'

'Well – you know she said I was too good for the soft-drink job, and she got me an audition for an Ibsen thing.'

'Yeah.'

'I went the other day. It was a disaster.'

'Why?'

'I just realized that the whole vibe in the previous audition was . . . you know . . . when I saw her sitting there in the rehearsal room, waiting for me, it hit me for the first time that . . . that . . . I mean, the woman's a beast. She's old. And this was just dawning on me when I realized that there was no one else around. No other actors waiting outside; no other people in the room; just me and her. Then she saw me, leapt up, kissed me on both cheeks, and gave me this scene for us to act out together. And it's a heavy love scene.'

'What? Shagging?'

'You haven't read much Ibsen, have you?'

'Er . . . no.'

'Not shagging – just lots of looking deep into each other's eyes and declaring eternal love for one another, then discussing how awful life is and how we want to die. I didn't have to physically *do* anything with her.

It was just – instead of reading her lines off the page like they normally do, she'd memorized her part, and she was saying all this love stuff as if she actually . . . you know . . . felt it.'

'You mean she was acting?'

'No. Well . . . yes. I mean, it would have been weird enough if she had been acting, since that's not what casting directors normally do, but she wasn't acting. It was like she meant it. And then I had to say it back as if *I* meant it, because I *was* supposed to be acting. And I wanted the part. You see what I mean?'

'Sort of.'

'So by the end of it, we're all heated and passionate together, and it's all really exciting, except for the fact that I'd been acting and she hadn't. She genuinely seems to think I love her. And she still doesn't know if I'm any good at acting. Which I'd just proved I was, since I'd made her think I loved her. But she doesn't know that, because she doesn't think I've been acting. So I'm now in a massive dilemma because I couldn't tell whether I stood more chance of getting the part by having her think I love her – so she gives it to me as a favour – or getting the part because she thinks I'm a good actor and have convincingly pretended to love her. I mean, she's a casting director. She's powerful. It's really important that she knows I'm a good actor.'

'So what did you do?'

'Well – I mean – I didn't have very long to think

about it, but I made a quick assessment of the situation, and decided that the best thing would be to tell the truth. That way I'd get out of the embarrassing situation of her coming on to me, and at the same time prove to her how good I am at my job. So after we'd done the scene, and she was fluttering her eyes at me, and I was getting all freaked out, I said to her that I'd been acting. She said, "I know you were", but still in this lovey-dovey way, as if she didn't believe me. So I said, "It really was acting. I don't find you at all attractive. I'm just a good actor. I think you're really ugly, and that shows how good I'll be in the part."'

'You said *that*?'

'Yeah. I'd just done this great performance, *in front of a casting director*, and she hadn't even noticed.'

'So you decided the best way to impress her was to tell her how ugly she is.'

'I wasn't thinking. It just came out wrong. I didn't mean to be rude.'

'You didn't mean to be rude?'

'I didn't realize how bad it would sound.'

'So what did she do? She chuck you out?'

'No. She started crying.'

'Really?'

'Yeah. Full-on sobbing. So I thought – you know, fair's fair – it's partly my fault – the least I can do is reciprocate what she did for me, so I gave her a hug and stroked her back while she wept away and told me how awful her marriage was and how miserable her life had become and how she loved me and lots of stuff like that.'

'She loves you?'

'Yeah. Then she told me the whole Ibsen thing was a set-up, and the play didn't exist, and she just wanted to spend more time with me.'

'What? You're joking!'

'No. I swear.'

'So what did you say?'

'Well – I'd already told her she was ugly. I didn't want to upset her any more. So I just said it didn't matter, and went along with the whole thing.'

'Why?'

'And we're going out for a meal next Thursday.'

'You're going out for a meal with her? But you think she's a beast! She sexually harassed you!'

'She's not a beast. She's just a bit old.'

'You said she was a beast.'

'I feel sorry for her. Her husband sounds like a real bastard.'

'It's not your problem.'

'That's a really bad attitude, Guy.'

'It's not an attitude. It's a fact.'

'If I can cheer her up just by eating with her . . .'

'She set you up. She's not your problem.'

'There's no *problem*, Guy. I'm just eating some food with her. It's no big deal.'

'Then why are you telling me you're so upset?'

'Well if you'd let me get a word in edgeways . . .'

'You've been talking all evening . . .'

'If you'd let me get a word in edgeways . . .'

'Yes . . .'

'What I've been trying to tell you is, the whole thing's got really difficult, because I've met someone else.'

'Already? Who?'

'This girl. I met her at a bus stop. I can't get her out of my head.'

'You're . . . how d'you meet someone at a bus stop?'

'We just got chatting. She's gorgeous.'

'You got chatting to a gorgeous girl at a bus stop?'

'Yeah.'

'How? What's gorgeous about her?'

'She's just pretty. And friendly. And she wears the most amazing clothes.'

'Since when are you interested in clothes?'

'It was this really kinky, slightly cross-dressy, semi-formal kind of outfit that was just *so* horny.'

'A kinky, cross-dressy, semi-formal kind of outfit?'

'You know – a shirt with a V-necked sweater, and a funny little skirt, then a man's jacket on top.'

'What – like school uniform?'

'Yeah.'

'School uniform?'

'Maybe, yeah.'

'She was wearing school uniform?'

63

'I hadn't thought of it like that, but . . . it could be that. Yeah.'

'For fuck's sake, Graham.'

'What?'

'Just . . . really . . .'

'What?'

'You're lusting after a schoolgirl?'

'Not lusting. I just found her attractive, that's all.'

'This is illegal. I could get you arrested.'

'I don't want to have sex with her, or anything.'

'Of course you don't.'

'I don't. She's a schoolgirl, for fuck's sake. I'm not a pervert.'

'You *are* a pervert.'

'No I'm not.'

'You are. Ever since Zoe chucked you, you've been fixated on the weirdest women. First it's a geriatric, then it's a schoolgirl – you're always going on about lesbians – you're a fucking pervert.'

'Look – if you're trying to tell me you've never had a lesbian fantasy . . .'

'Graham – listen to me. Forget the schoolgirl. Forget the pensioner. You're ill. You're on the rebound. Your testosterone's been poisoned. Just . . . I think you should stay out of polite society until you've got your head together, then . . . you know . . . when you stop thinking like a sicko you can go out into the world again and start looking for someone new. You're acting like an arsehole. You've got to grow up.'

Graham stares at Guy, his eyes filling with tears (a trick he learnt in drama school). He takes a few slow sips of beer. 'Thanks,' he says, quietly.

'What?'

'Thanks.'

'What for?'

'Just . . . you're right. You're absolutely right. You're my best mate and you always tell me the truth and I love you for it.'

'Please, Graham – don't go all maudlin on me.'

'However much it hurts, you'll come out and say it.'

'Graham . . .'

'Regardless of the pain it will cause, like a true friend, you'll take your sword of truth and stab it into me. Several times. In the kidneys. Then into my neck.'

'Don't be like this.'

'No – I appreciate it, Guy. I really do. You're a good friend.'

'Look –. . .'

'I wouldn't want a friend who felt the need to lie. I don't want pity. Or compassion. Or concern.'

'I'm concerned, Graham. Of course I'm concerned.'

'THEN STOP TEARING ME TO SHREDS, YOU FUCKING WANKER!'

'I'm not. I didn't mean to. I'm just . . . you know . . . I've been worried about you and I'm trying to help.'

'Telling me I'm an arsehole and I have to grow up is not what I call help.'

'I didn't mean it as a criticism.'

'Oh, it was *praise*?'

'I just think that you've been acting strangely lately, and someone's got to say something to stop you getting obsessed with weird women, and help you get back to . . . you know . . . normality.'

'That's what you were trying to do?'

'Yes!'

'Help me get a normal girlfriend?'

'Yes.'

'Go on, then.'

'What?'

'Do it.'

'Do what?'

'Help me get a girlfriend. You know loads of single women. Introduce me to someone.'

'If that's what you want.'

'Of course it's what I want.'

'If you think you're ready . . .'

'What about that one you're always talking about? The sexy depressive one. I like the sound of her.'

'She's not sexy.'

'Of course she is. If she wasn't horny, you wouldn't go on about her so much.'

'She's not your type.'

'It's worth a go.'

'She's one of my best friends, Graham.'

'Perfect.'

'She's my *friend*. If you're acting all fucked up, I'm

not going to try and set you up with someone I care about.'

'She's too good for me?'

'No.'

'You're saying she's too good for me?'

'I'm not.'

'Then introduce me to her.'

'No.'

'*Why not?*'

'Because ... OK ... because she's too good for you.'

'How can you say that?'

'Because it's true.'

'I'm your oldest friend!'

'That doesn't mean you're not a weirdo.'

'Guy – I just want to meet her for a drink. You can come. I'm not going to ravish her. It's just a bit of basic social interaction with a single person of a vaguely different gender. It's not a lot to ask. If she doesn't like me, then she doesn't like me. That's cool. You've slagged me off all evening with the excuse that you're trying to help, and if you can't even do this for me ... if you won't even help me make this tiny little step in the right direction, then you're ... you're ... a wanker.'

'Don't make such a big deal out of it.'

'You're the one making a big deal out of it. I'm asking for a simple little drink with a friend of yours, and you're turning it into some hugely significant event I can't even be trusted with.'

'OK! OK! We can go for a drink. But if you . . . if anything happens and you treat her badly, I'll kill you.'

'I've never treated a woman badly in my life. It's them who treat me badly.'

'That's what they all say.'

'It's true. You know it's true.'

'Just . . . be careful. This is serious. She isn't a joke.'

'Fine.'

'Fine. And she might not even be interested.'

'But you'll ask?'

'I'll ask.'

'And you won't tell her I'm a freak.'

'I won't tell her you're a freak.'

'You promise?'

'Promise. I'll ask.'

9

By the time Keri was leaving for work the next day she had forgotten all about Josh, and it therefore came as rather a surprise to find him sitting in her front garden.

'Jesus! What are you doing here?'

'Waiting for you,' says Josh, with a nervous smile.

'Why?'

'So I could see you.'

'Why?'

Josh stands and walks towards her. Keri tries not to flinch.

'I just think we need to clear up the situation between us, so we both know where we stand,' he says. This was the core of Josh's meticulously prepared declaration of love, which in rehearsal consisted of several moving and mature-sounding paragraphs. In performance it had come out rather stunted.

'What situation between us?'

'I just think we should clarify . . .'

'Is it not clear? Can't you understand that I don't want to see you again?'

'Look – Keri – I understand that you're angry with me, but when that subsides, we have to take a look at what happened between us and try to salvage something positive.'

'Nothing *happened* between us, Josh.'

'We'll never get anywhere if you just react angrily like this all the time.'

'I'm not angry. I just never want to see you again.'

'Look – if you're not angry, why are you always raising your voice and telling me you never want to see me again?'

'Because I don't like you? Because I regret every second I spend with you? Things like that.'

'If we could just . . .'

'Josh! Did you not hear me? I don't like you! I find you physically repulsive! End of story!'

Staring into Keri's eyes, Josh's brain suddenly executes a stomach-churning U-turn as it dawns on him that she means what she's saying. He hadn't done something to upset her. She wasn't waiting for him to make amends. She just didn't like him.

He feels his body shrink inside his skin, and his eyes lose focus.

Keri watches Josh's face change colour, like a Polaroid in reverse, as blood drains from his features. With every muscle in Josh's body paralysed, Keri finds herself unable to walk away – inhibited by curiosity, guilt, and the fear that he was having a genuine seizure.

Swaying slightly, Josh gradually comes back to life. Clearing his throat, he mumbles, 'Really?'

Keri, avoiding his gaze, doesn't answer.

'You find me physically repulsive?' he says.

Keri strains to think of an answer which is reassuring enough to get her out of the conversation, but cold enough to ensure that he leaves her alone. A long silence yawns between them.

With Josh's swelling eyes beaming a needy glare toward her, she looks up and forces a thin smile to her lips. 'Maybe not *repulsive*. That's too strong. Just ... you know ... unpleasant,' she says, encouragingly.

Josh sniffs, his nose reddening under the pressure of suppressed sobs. 'Unpleasant?'

'Unpleasant. That's all.'

'Why? What's wrong with me?'

'Nothing. Nothing's wrong with you.'

'So why am I physically unpleasant?'

'Not ... in general ... Just to me. It's a personal thing.'

'Is it how I look? Or what I do?'

'Neither ... I mean, both ... Just ... Well ...' Keri's feelings of guilt, which have already transmuted into embarrassment, now begin to swerve back towards anger. 'Look,' she continues, 'it's not my problem. You can't ask questions like that. No one asks questions like that. You can't expect me to ... to ...'

'Just tell me. I have to know. Then I'll leave you alone. Just answer the question, and ... and I'll never get in your way again.'

Keri sighs.

'Is it how I look?'

The offer of a permanent release from Josh's attentions is deeply tempting. Keri looks up, and stares at him expressionlessly. Suppressing an urge to slap him, she finally answers. 'You look fine, Josh. You're a good-looking guy. Now I have to get to work.'

'So it's what I do?'

'Josh . . .'

'It's what I do? You think I'm bad in bed.'

'I have to get to . . .'

'Am I bad in bed?'

'Look – you said you'd leave me alone if I answered the question.'

'You haven't answered. The question was, "Is it how I look or what I do?"'

'That's two questions.'

'It's one question. Just tell me, and I'll leave you alone.'

'Josh – what's your fucking problem? What do you want from me?'

'Just tell me – am I a bad person or a bad lover?'

'You want to know?'

'Yes.'

'You really want to know?'

'Yes.'

'The truth?'

'Yes.'

'You sure?'

'Yes.'

'OK. The answer is: both. On a personal level you are self-regarding, vain, ignorant and unimaginative. In bed, you are self-regarding, vain, ignorant, unimaginative, and lacking in technique.'

Josh stares at her, physically immobilized. He blinks. No other muscle in his body moves.

'Can I go now?' says Keri.

Josh still doesn't move, and Keri takes advantage of his temporary paralysis to walk round him, squeezing through the gateway of her front garden.

As she marches off to the Tube station, she hears the muffled thump of skull hitting concrete. Josh, it seems, has passed out.

Keri glances at her watch and quickens her pace.

*　　*　　*

Lisa's work, for once, was going well. For eighteen months she had been intermittently tinkering with a Celebrities and their Bathrooms project for ITV, and now, at last, Network Centre had issued the first glimmers of interest.

This was both exciting and worrying for Lisa, since she couldn't help suspecting that the main selling-point of the programme was its presenter, Dawn French. It was Lisa who had put this name down on the proposal in a moment of . . . well, optimism. What Dawn French's agent had actually said was, 'Dawn's busy until 2003, but try again when you've got a commission. You never know your luck.'

Now ITV wanted to spend money on researching celebrities with interesting bathrooms, and Lisa would have to contact Dawn French's agent to remind her of the fifteen-second phone call they'd had nine months previously and to 'check that Dawn was still interested'. Which, obviously, she wouldn't be.

Still, if Lisa could find enough interesting bathrooms with ITV's extra money, then maybe she could slip the idea through without anyone noticing that it was now presented by someone along the lines of . . . say, Kris Akabusi.

Any interest from a broadcaster, however much it was founded on fantasy, constituted progress, and the response from ITV had put Geoff into what could almost be called a good mood. Lisa, too, would have been happier than usual, had it not been for a creeping anxiety about Josh's unexplained absence from the office.

As the morning progressed Lisa became increasingly worried.

At eleven-thirty, she dials his home.

'Hi. We're not here. But — hell — that's what answerphones are for. Beeeep.'

'It's me,' says Lisa. 'Just wondering where you are. Call me at work if you get this. Bye.'

Lisa hangs up, now feeling perturbed not only by

Josh's disappearance, but also by the fact that he comes across as a pompous jerk on his answerphone message.

She picks up her receiver again and calls Spotlight, dialling from memory.

'Hi,' she says. 'I'm trying to find a number for Kris Akabusi's agent.'

'Please hold . . .'

10

Guy liked to think of himself as ruthlessly ambitious. But he wasn't. After finishing his degree he had pissed around for a while, then, having failed to decide what he wanted to do with his life, he went back to university and did an M A. He then pissed around a bit more, still couldn't decide what he wanted to do, and soon found himself back at university doing a Ph.D.

Now, half-way through the fourth year of a Ph.D., he was within sight of his thirties, and still hadn't applied for his first job. In theory, he wanted to be rich and successful. He just hadn't got round to that part of his life-plan yet. He had tried to concentrate on being happy first, with the intention that after he had this sorted out, he could focus on the wealth and success bit. Several years into this scheme, phase one was still eluding him.

By now, he was overqualified for a normal job, but didn't want to work in academia because he hated academics. And universities. And students.

There is a term in career handbooks for Guy's position. He's fucked.

Staring into his computer screen, he is suddenly brought to his senses when the text vanishes and a screensaver of flying windows flashes into view. This means he hasn't touched the keyboard for five minutes. He presses the space bar and looks at his watch. Six-thirty. Time to stop. Or it would be time to stop, if his day's work had started more than two hours ago. Which it hadn't.

He does a quick word-count. 73,472 words. 326,119 characters. That's a lot of work, he thinks. Three and a half years to push 326,119 buttons. Or maybe it's not very much work at all. He's had more than a thousand days. Seventy-three words a day really isn't very much at all. It's almost nothing. It's the equivalent of stopping for a cup of tea between every single letter.

Most significantly, 73,472 words is only two hundred words more than yesterday. Guy closes his eyes and allows his head to slump on to the desk, adding the word 'jdhrtbbj6hfdtr' to the end of his Ph.D. Then he sits up, and without consciously deciding to do so, types, 'what a waste of a lif'.

He swears at himself, deletes 'jdhrtbbj6hfdtr what a waste of a lif', and resolves to carry on working until Lisa gets home.

Two hours later, Guy has written one more paragraph, and Lisa still hasn't arrived. He switches off his computer, and tries to think where she might be. Then he suddenly remembers that she could be anywhere, and wouldn't have rung since he had told her that he'd be in the pub with Graham and Helen. Which he would be, if he hadn't forgotten about the entire thing. It's now eight-thirty, and Guy is more than an hour late.

He rushes to the kitchen, slices off a hunk of bread, slaps a slice of salami on to it, throws on his coat, walks back to the kitchen, opens and closes the fridge a few times, puts an apple in his pocket and rushes out of the door.

*   *   *

Graham deliberately chooses an unwarped table. After all, this is almost a date. He has to be cool, keep his elbows dry, and generally try to impress Helen. He has arrived early to give himself time to select the right table, settle in, and calm his nerves.

After fifteen minutes, he's bored. Neither Helen or Guy has arrived. Then a short woman with dark hair and an on-the-verge-of-tears face walks in. Graham knows it's her. He watches her glance around the room, using his anonymity to have a good stare. She looks O K. Not beautiful – but O K.

Helen sees him staring in her direction and squints at him, pulling a do-I-know-you? face. Graham stands up and gives a little no-you-don't-but-I-am-the-person-you're-looking-for wave. She walks over, hesitantly, and sticks her arm out for a handshake just as Graham leans toward her for a kiss on the cheek. He bobs back as fast as he can, trying to eradicate the impression that he had tried to kiss her, almost loses his balance, and steadies himself against the table.

He takes her hand, which feels rather like an old piece of lettuce, and shakes it as gently as he can for fear of breaking it. 'Helen?' he says.

'Yes. Graham?'

'Yup. You want a . . . ?'

'Please. Beer.'

'Bottle? Pint?'

'Bottle.'

'Any . . . er . . . ?'

'Whatever.'

'Becks?'

'Great.'

'O K.'

Graham walks to the bar, rattling the coins in his pocket, suddenly tense.

He places a Becks in front of her, sits, and smiles.

'Guy's . . . er . . . ?' she says.

He shrugs. 'Not . . .'

'Here yet?'

'No.'

'Late. Probably. As usual.'

'As usual,' he says, smiling.

She smiles back. 'He'll . . . shouldn't be . . . long.'

'Sentences,' he says. 'You don't believe in them?'

A flicker of life springs into her eyes. 'Sometimes,'

79

she says, smirking. 'Sometimes useful. Unnecessary often.'

'Word order? Find it useful you don't?'

Helen smiles again. She had been dreading the evening, knowing that Guy would contrive to leave her alone with a complete stranger. Graham seemed OK, though. You could instantly spot him as the kind of person who wasn't remotely interested in having a serious conversation, and it was a relief to be able to talk nonsense, instead of going through the usual what-do-you-do? where-do-you-live? do-you-like-it-there? conversation she always seemed to have at parties. Graham, it was already clear, was only interested in nonsense.

'Word order,' she says, surprised by the sudden loudness of her own voice, 'meaning for the communication of essential sometimes. But unnecessary often.'

Graham laughs. 'Guy fucking bastard late for being is. Introduced us hasn't even.'

'Bastard fucking. Right are you.'

By means of this strange and ludicrously extended joke, Graham and Helen spend the next hour in a conspiratorially incomprehensible conversation involving ever-more-bizarre speech patterns. By the time Guy finally arrives, Graham and Helen have managed to discover what each other does, where they live, and whether they like it there, all without boring one another.

'Bastard fucking!' says Graham pointing at the door.

'Where?' says Helen.

'Door by the.'

'Door by the?'

'Look don't! Hour late bastard fucking! Hide let's.'

'Hide let's? From bastard fucking?'

'Table under!' says Graham.

Helen grins and dives under the table. Just in time to avoid catching Guy's eye, Graham also slips under the table, in the process banging Helen's head with his knee.

'Ow!'

'Shit. Sorry.'

'Knee you face me in the hit!'

'Rub it can I better?'

Helen takes Graham's hand and places it above her eyebrow. She holds the back of his hand as he rubs, both of them laughing so much that the table shakes, rattling their glasses.

'Hurt it does?' he says.

'Really not. Really not . . . SHIT!'

'What?'

'Bar staff what if glasses take our gone thinking we're.'

'Say that again?'

'Bar staff what if glasses take our gone thinking we're. Idiot.'

'Bastards fucking! Glasses taking!? Quick.'

Graham reaches an arm up and pats the top of the table, seeking out their glasses. He finds his beer, and brings it under the table, passing it to Helen. She grins and takes a sip. He then reaches up on the far side of the table, which involves sprawling all over Helen. She doesn't seem to mind, however, and it even occurs to Graham that she is deliberately positioning her body to make it awkward for him to squeeze past. Eventually, he finds her bottle and hands it to her.

She takes the bottle, and drinks from that, too. With a bottle of beer in one hand, a pint in the other, and the underside of a pub table squashing her head to a funny angle, it occurs to Graham that Helen is magnificently sexy.

He tries to think this thought privately, but as soon as he has thought it, he realizes that he has given out his realization as a sexual vibe. He sees Helen receiving the message, and registers a slight frown on her face: a frown that is somehow both flirtatious and cold. Graham doesn't know what this look means, and he allows the silence to grow between them, sensing that if they weren't underneath a table, an attempted kiss would be the most sensible course of action.

Helen is still holding his gaze when they hear Guy's voice, just above their heads. 'What are you doing?' he says.

Graham and Helen creep out from under the table, looking flushed and guilty.

'What are you down there for?' he says.

'Er . . . accident,' says Graham. 'Slippage. From the chairs.'

Helen laughs. Guy shakes his head. He gives Graham an inquisitive stare, but Graham looks away and catches Helen's eye.

Guy's guilt at being late has evaporated. He now simply feels annoyed at being excluded from a private joke between two of his closest friends who aren't supposed even to know each other.

Realizing that this is juvenile, he forces a smile. 'Sorry I'm late,' he says, without much sincerity. 'You two want a drink?'

Graham nods. Helen nods.

'Same again?' says Guy.

They both nod.

Guy turns and walks to the bar. Alcohol, he decides, is what he needs. A quick shot of whisky at the bar is probably the best way to douse his annoyance. *Cheer up*, he tells himself. *Make yourself cheer up.*

Although the couple of hours remaining until closing time weren't exactly fun, Helen felt intensely happy. She loved Guy as a loyal and sympathetic friend, but there was something about the way he treated her that she found annoying. He always made an effort to be gentle and understanding with her, in a way which half the time she adored but the rest of the time seemed cloying and oppressive.

It was as if Guy preferred to spend time with her when she was miserable – as if she was letting him down on occasions when she just wanted to have a laugh. Guy also never gave anything away about his own problems, and as a result their friendship was frustratingly unequal.

When Helen felt bad, Guy was always the first person she wanted to see. During her lows – of which there were many – she often thought he was the only person she knew who genuinely cared about her. When she was feeling strong, however, Guy annoyed her. He never took her happiness seriously, and often patronized her, as if only the miserable Helen was the real her. He always brought home to her the fleeting nature of her moods, which, when she felt good, was the last thing she wanted to think about.

The more he went out of his way to bolster her self-esteem, the more he undermined her. He reduced her to the status of a victim, and for this she resented him.

Sitting in the pub with Guy and Graham, it dawned on her that Guy had never really seen her being silly before. He had never seen her being funny. And the more she pissed around with Graham, the more Guy seemed ill at ease, which just made her want to be more and more silly. She was proving something to Guy. *Look*, she was saying. *I'm not just what you think I am. I'm like this. And you don't like the fact that this is also me.*

Helen could tell Guy felt threatened, and she loved that sensation. This was her way of letting Guy know that he held her back. The more she laughed and flirted with Graham, the more she felt she was teaching Guy a lesson – showing him who she really was – and if he couldn't handle that, then he wasn't a true friend.

The three of them hover on the pavement outside the pub after chucking-out time. Helen turns to Guy and says, in an ostentatiously cheerful voice, 'Are you going home?'

'Er . . . yeah,' he says.

'You walking?'

'Yeah.'

'And you?' says Helen, to Graham. 'You going home? Or do you want to come back to mine for a coffee?'

Graham swallows, and coughs. This invitation is blatantly addressed to him alone. He knows he mustn't look at Guy.

'It's not far,' she says. 'We can bus it.'

'Err . . . OK,' he says.

Helen takes Graham's arm and smiles falsely at Guy, who looks at her, holding a searching stare for a few seconds, before turning away wordlessly and wandering off with his hands in his pockets and his head down.

Helen and Graham watch him walk away in silence.

'What's that about?' says Graham, in a half-whisper.

'What?' says Helen, still smiling.

'That wasn't very friendly.'

Helen turns to Graham, her eyes shining with excitement. She stares at him, and he has no idea what she will say next. Suddenly, she starts jumping up and down on the spot. Three jumps – and with each one, she kisses him on the cheek.

'You think I'm not friendly?' she asks, her voice ringing with fearlessly intense happiness.

Oh, fuck, thinks Graham. *This girl's a nutter.*

'You're friendly,' he says, kissing her gently on the lips. 'You're very friendly.'

Hand in hand, they walk to the bus stop.

From earliest childhood, one of Graham's defining characteristics has been his cowardice. When called upon, this feature of his psychological make-up would usually let him know exactly how to respond to any potentially frightening situation. Being dragged by the arm up the stairs to Helen's flat, his instincts were failing him, sending conflicting messages, ranging from 'RUN!' to 'PLAY ALONG WITH IT!' to 'PLAY DEAD!'.

Inside the living room of her flat, Helen indicates to Graham to be quiet, then immediately tiptoes out of view. She returns noisily, wearing a big grin.

'She's not here,' says Helen, with a hint of sal-
aciousness.

'Who?'

'Flatmate. She must be at her boyfriend's.'

'Oh, right,' says Graham. 'Good.'

They stare at each other, and Graham gets the
feeling that Helen is giving him a shall-we-get-right-
down-to-it-or-would-you-prefer-a-bit-more-conver-
sation? look.

'I quite fancy a . . .'

'Drink,' she says. 'What do you want to drink?'

'Have you got any . . . er . . . tea?'

At the sound of the word 'tea', Helen's eyes seem
to dim slightly.

'Tea?' she says. 'What kind of tea?'

'You got any . . . herbal?'

'Herbal,' she says, sounding pissed off. 'I'll have a
look.' With that, she leaves the room, and Graham
hears the noisy clattering of kitchen cupboards.

He doesn't really want a cup of tea. Helen knows
he doesn't want a cup of tea. Just by asking for
a lust-free hot drink, instead of more alcohol, it is
suddenly clear that the brakes have been applied to
their flirtation.

Graham sits on the sofa, listening to the rumbling
kettle, trying to gauge Helen's mood by the fridge,
footstep and cupboard noises which are wafting into
the living room. She definitely sounds pissed off.

*

Sitting next to each other on the sofa, sipping at tea which has no flavour and scalds, Graham wonders what on earth he's doing in this woman's flat. All he did was ask for tea – it was hardly the most brutal insult he'd ever dished out – and suddenly they had nothing to say to one another. All the tea request had meant was that he didn't quite feel ready to immediately leap into her bed. It didn't mean that he wasn't willing. In fact, now that he'd had a bit of time with her, over a cup of tea, and it had been established that they had nothing more of interest to say to one another, it became more obvious than ever that the only thing to do was to have sex.

Unfortunately, he'd ruined the momentum. The tea had been a terrible idea. If he'd asked for a whisky, he could have had a bit of time to catch his breath, and to check that she wasn't *too* much of a psycho, and somehow he wouldn't have stopped the whole thing in its tracks. Now, it felt as if they'd just met each other. He was back at square one.

Just as his tea was reaching a drinkable temperature, Graham resolved that he definitely did want to sleep with her. He just didn't know how. A minute ago, it had been obvious. She was looking at him in a shag-me way, and he could easily have just . . . well, shagged her. All he would have had to do was throw himself at her, and the whole thing would have just happened.

Now, they were sitting next to each other on a sofa,

drinking hot drinks, she wasn't talking or looking at him, they were miles from the bedroom, and they were fully clothed. There seemed to be such a long distance between near-silent living-room embarrassment and hot, wet bedroom fucking, that he simply couldn't figure out how to get from one to the other. The clothing seemed a particularly insuperable obstacle. How were you supposed to get the other person's clothes off? With clothes on, you couldn't really get to any respectable level of lustful activity, but until you had reached at least some degree of passion, how could you set about removing their clothes? You couldn't just take a mug out of their hands, put it on the coffee-table, and set about untying their shoelaces. It didn't work like that.

He knew that the next step was just to kiss her, but she didn't seem to want to be kissed. And even if he did manage to kiss her, the mountain of obstacles between that and getting her into bed suddenly seemed off-puttingly huge. The whole thing felt like such an enormously complex task, strewn with pitfalls, potential embarrassments, and the liability of biological let-down that Graham began to feel he didn't have the stomach for it. He was just that little bit too tired. Maybe half an hour ago he would have been up to it, but now it was just too late. It all seemed like too much effort.

On the other hand, not shagging her was probably now even more embarrassing than trying to shag her.

There was simply no way he could just finish his tea, shake her hand, and leave. Besides, he now felt randy. No – this wasn't the time to consider tiredness. He had to stop fretting, and do something. He wanted sex. He was alone with a woman, in her flat, and even though she was temporarily quiet and sulky, she had spent the majority of the evening acting as if she wanted him. This kind of opportunity didn't exactly come along every day. He'd be an idiot if he didn't at least attempt to get something out of it. In fact, he'd be clinically insane if he left without having a try.

It was time to stop thinking and go for it – to kiss her, and then just let the whole thing happen. Or not happen. Either way, he had to kiss her.

Helen, meanwhile, couldn't figure out what Graham was thinking. Everything had been going fine until suddenly, for no apparent reason, he had insisted on sending her into the kitchen for a cup of camomile tea. What *else* did he want? A hot-water bottle?

The instant he asked for his tea, the surge of flirtation which had carried her through the entire evening suddenly halted. The unreality, the thrill of acting out an evening that you know is a story – the best story – a sex story – abruptly evaporated. Something in the way he asked, and in the nature of his request, injected the dead weight of the real world back into her mind, making her question, for the first time, whether or not he fancied her.

The presence of this doubt altered everything. Her self-confidence slipped away. Her lust dried up. She noticed that Graham wasn't particularly good-looking. And she remembered that she had been staggeringly rude to Guy. The evening had been a disaster.

Yet again, she had mistaken a no one for an ally, and had alienated someone she cared about. However many times she did this, however often she vowed to be less hasty to switch allegiances, she never learnt. She was an idiot. She hated herself.

By the time the kettle boiled, she had almost forgotten who the second cup was for. As soon as he finished his drink, she wanted Graham out. She should never have invited him back to her flat. She wanted to be alone. She wanted to collect her thoughts, phone Guy, and explain to him why she had behaved so badly.

He'd understand – he always understood – but for her own self-respect she had to apologize as soon as possible. She wanted him to know that her behaviour had been a fleeting aberration, and she had got herself back under control without doing anything stupid. She wanted him to know that she was sorry. She wanted him to know that she hadn't slept with Graham.

Just as it looks like Graham is beginning to make a serious attempt to consume some of his tea, he suddenly stops drinking, places his mug on the coffee-table, and launches himself at Helen. She doesn't even have time to put down her drink before Graham's rough chin is scrabbling around her face, attempting to ferret out a little lip-to-lip contact. Hot tea spills over her hand, causing her to yelp in pain.

'Ow! What the fuck are you doing?'

Struck dumb, Graham withdraws to the far corner of the sofa.

'Christ!' says Helen.

Graham stands up, a head-rush of embarrassment almost causing him to fall over. His timing was appalling. He had thrown himself at her without even establishing eye contact first. His approach had been less subtle than that of an average mugger. Besides, he really didn't want to have sex with her. This was now obvious. He was just having a go – to see what happened – to find out if she still wanted him. Clearly, she didn't.

'I'll leave,' he says. 'Sorry. I like you, but . . . forget it. Let's pretend this never happened.'

'Fine,' says Helen. 'Whatever.'

Graham tries to give her a friendly smile on the way out, but she won't even look at him.

Helen, in fact, won't look at him in case she finds herself breaking into a smile. The only way she could sustain her outraged appearance was to keep staring at the floor. She had shouted at him simply because he caught her by surprise. She literally hadn't seen him coming, and he had given her a fright by suddenly appearing in her face without any warning. Then, having seen his mortified and embarrassed reaction, she realized that she had unwittingly set in motion emergency procedures for getting him out of the flat. All she had to do was look at the carpet, and Graham's humiliation would propel him through the front door.

When she hears the latch of the outside door click shut, she almost whoops with relief. She checks her watch. It is too late to ring Guy, so she slumps on to the sofa and flicks on the TV.

11

Lisa arrives home to find the flat empty. Remembering that Guy is on one of his mop-up-Helen's-tears evenings, she immediately picks up the phone and rings Josh. The answerphone is still on.

'Josh,' she says. 'Pick up. I know you're there. You're hiding. I know you are. Just pick up the phone, you arsehole, so I know you're all right. Josh . . .'

Lisa hears a click, then a groan, before a groggy-sounding voice whimpers from the earpiece, 'Lisa?'

'Josh? Are you OK?'

'I'm ill. I fell ill.'

'Why didn't you call in?'

'Because I'm *ill*.'

'I've been worried.'

'Well, I've been ill.'

'Why didn't you pick up any of my calls?'

'I wasn't here.'

'So you're too ill to come to work, or to phone me, but not too ill to be out all day.'

'I was at the hospital, Lisa. OK?'

'Hospital? What's wrong? What happened?'

'It's nothing.'

'Josh – tell me.'

'It's nothing, honestly. Just a bit of concussion.'

'Concussion? How?'

'How did I get concussion?'

'Yeah.'

Josh thinks for a moment, attempting to sound traumatized and pensive rather than simply at a loss.

'Mugging. I was mugged,' he says, sharply.

'When?'

'On . . . on the way to work. This morning.'

'In the morning? You were mugged in the morning?'

'Yeah. I just got jumped. By this really big bloke. Two of them. Massive. And they hit me round the head and ran off with my money.'

'Shit. I'm coming round.'

'Don't.'

'I am. I'm on my way.'

'Lisa – don't. Really. I just . . . need to sleep. I don't feel good.'

'Did you . . . have you . . . been to the police?'

'Er . . . yeah. Like I said – I was at the hospital and the police station all day, and I've just got back and I want to sleep.'

'Are you sure you're OK?'

'Yeah. Sort of. I was unconscious for quite a while.'

'*Unconscious?* What did they hit you with?'

'A thing . . . a big thing . . . a bat . . . baseball bat.'

'That's awful! You sure you don't want me to pop in?'

'Positive.'

'You staying home tomorrow as well?'

'Er . . . yeah. That's a good idea. Will you tell Geoff what happened?'

'Sure. Sure.'

'You think he'll be OK about it?'

'He'll just have to be, won't he? Anyway – he's in a good mood. ITV want the bathrooms thing.'

'Really?'

'Yeah. Dawn French's agent says she'll sue us if we ever use her name without permission again, but basically it looks like we might have got away with it.'

'That's good.'

'Are you sure you're OK?'

'I just have to sleep. I'll be fine.'

'OK.'

'And well done. On the bathrooms thing.'

'Thanks. And you.'

'And me? Well done for getting mugged?'

'Something like that. Sorry. Don't know what I'm talking about.'

Josh chuckles, which hurts his head.

'Bye, then,' he says, and hangs up, impressed with himself for having come up with such a convincing lie to conceal his situation. It hadn't even occurred to him to think of taking an extra day off, but he now realized this was exactly what he needed. He wasn't yet ready to face humanity again.

He shuffles to his bedroom, contemplates the notion of getting undressed, but gives up after a couple of shirt buttons and flops on to the mattress. He closes his eyes and instantly falls asleep, his brain, sinuses, eyeballs and teeth throbbing a symphony of pain.

Lisa's hand is still on the telephone, and she is about to dial Keri in search of a bit more information about what might have really happened to Josh, when Guy stumbles noisily into the flat.

He lunges towards her, and grabs her round the waist. She tries to wriggle free, but he doesn't let go.

'Get off!' she says. 'What are you doing?'

'Nothing.'

They stare at one another, slightly too close to be able to focus properly. Guy thinks about kissing her, but she is still pulling her what's-wrong-with-you? face. He tries to smile, but it's pretty clear that Lisa isn't in the mood to be fondled by a quarter-pissed boyfriend, so he releases her from his hug. She squirms away from him, scowling.

'I'm almost pissed,' he says, opting for honesty. 'It's the worst stage. You're just beginning to get the urge to lose your inhibitions, but you haven't actually lost them yet.'

'Couple more drinks, and you would have torn my clothes off and raped me, then?'

'I might have tried.'

'That's not funny.'

'What do you mean it's not funny? You're the one that said it.'

'I'm allowed to say it. You agreed with me, which isn't funny.'

'Oh. OK. Am I allowed to agree with you now?'

'About what?'

'Can I agree with you that I'm not allowed to agree with you?'

Lisa opens her mouth but can't think of a way to raise the facetiousness stakes and reaches for the TV remote-control. She flicks it on, and the pair of them slump on to the sofa. They stare blankly at the screen.

'Look,' says Guy, after a while. 'It's that bloke.'

'What bloke?'

'Him. He's so shit.'

Lisa immediately recognized Guy's aggressive randiness and moaning as two sure signs that he was not, in fact, drunk, but was in a bad mood. Guy was never honest about his moods. For some reason, he always considered it essential to hide one type of socially destructive mood behind another complementary mood of a similar variety. If he was upset, he'd pretend to be angry; if he was angry, he'd pretend to be pissed; and if he was pissed, he'd pretend to be deliriously happy.

He seemed to think it was unmanly to give any clear signals about what was going on in his head, yet would strive desperately to communicate his emotions via this complex procedure of encoding. The last thing he wanted was for no one to realize he was unhappy. It was, in fact, extremely important that everyone knew precisely how he felt – he just couldn't let on that he wanted anyone to know. Hence the complex mood disguises and decoy emotional outbursts.

Concluding from his behaviour that Guy is angry about something, Lisa sighs. She toys with the idea of pretending not to have decoded his mood, then thinks of acknowledging it and immediately leaving the room. She doesn't feel like active sympathizing. Besides, Guy's constant concealment of his emotions gets on her nerves, and the fact that he hasn't directly told her that he's pissed off absolves her from the obligation to ask him what's wrong.

She sits next to him, puts one hand on his thigh, and with the other, starts channel-hopping. 'Oh look,' she says, comfortingly. 'It's her. She's shit.'

'She's not. She's all right.'

'She's cross-eyed. She's shit.'

Guy looks at Lisa and smiles, gratefully. The beauty of a long relationship is that your partner always knows the best way to cheer you up. He doesn't feel like discussing Helen's awful behaviour, or Graham's betrayal. He had been feeling miserable about it all the way home, and had stamped into the flat hoping to start an argument. But now, here he was, watching telly with Lisa, suddenly and inexplicably happy.

So maybe he did have crap friends who were disloyal and utterly unworthy of him – so what? He had Lisa, who loved him and understood him and knew exactly when to put a hand on his leg and take the piss out of the TV with him.

In Lisa, he had what he needed. His life had changed. Friendship wasn't the most important thing any more. No one really looked out for anyone else. Everyone was more self-obsessed than ever before. The minute his friends had a shag on the horizon, they ditched him, only to come crawling back when they were alone again.

Guy was beginning to have had enough. He wanted to be treated fairly by his friends, but he suddenly saw that this simply wasn't going to happen. For the first time in his life, Guy could see why people became boring as they got older – why people retreated into couples. After a certain point, your friends just weren't loyal to you any more. As people took their lives increasingly seriously, they lost space in their minds for all but one other person. And single people lost space for everyone but themselves.

Whatever Graham or Helen did to him, he didn't really care any more. They weren't worth the effort. He had what he needed at home.

Guy wriggles his hand underneath Lisa's and squeezes, feeling a surge of gratitude for her presence in his life. 'She's not cross-eyed,' he says. 'If you think she's cross-eyed, you must be cross-eyed.'

Lisa smiles at him, crosses her eyes, and changes the channel.

12

Saturday morning. Josh wakes up to the sound of tweeting birds. He instantly remembers his last thought before falling asleep, which was that he would make an effort to sleep as far beyond midday as he could, in order to leave himself the smallest possible amount of Saturday in which he would have to be conscious. Now it was barely dawn, and he was already awake. Even if he managed to get to sleep before nightfall on Sunday, this still left him thirty-six hours of weekend to live through.

Thirty-six hours. Twelve video tapes. Allowing for a long sleep on Sunday, he could possibly get this down to nine. On the other hand, if he went for rented films, they would average less than two hours each, in which case he'd need at least fourteen films. But the rental shop didn't even open until eleven o'clock. Which cut the number of tapes down to twelve, but left him with five hours to kill. Though perhaps those five hours could be usefully employed choosing which films to hire.

A certain critical mass of epic weepies was essential, but if he went too far along that route he'd probably kill himself. A few Zucker brothers and Monty Python jobs would be necessary to counterbalance the misery.

On top of that, a healthy dose of ultraviolence was probably the best way to alleviate his depression. In fact, a good splatter movie was what he needed right away if he wanted to stand any chance of being able to face the world. A strong cup of tea and the heedless slaughter of a few sexually attractive American teenagers was exactly the thing.

Maybe that would have to provide the general theme of his dodecimal bill. Violence against women. This was the only way he was ever going to cheer himself up.

Josh decided that he had spent enough of his life pondering his own problems. He knew that there was nothing wrong with him. He was a good person. A decent-looking, decent-acting, reasonably intelligent nice guy. He was a nice guy. And yet at every turn, women had abused, undermined and humiliated him.

There was, quite simply, no justice to the way he had been treated. All his life he had been crippling himself with anxiety about what women thought of him, and now he had finally crossed a threshold. Never again would he allow himself to get into a position where some woman was going to be allowed to feel she had the key to *his* self-confidence.

He suddenly realized what an idiot he'd been. In tactical terms, over and over again, he had simply handed all the power to the enemy. He had always left it in their hands to decide the fate of any possible relationship. He had never given himself a chance. Every time, he had surrendered before the battle was even under way.

No wonder people like Keri could crush him so easily. He was pathetic. He had never shown any strength. He had never stamped his authority on a woman. His vulnerability invited women to spit in his face. The more desperate you were for a woman to like you, the less chance you stood of getting any genuine respect.

It was now utterly clear to Josh where he had been going wrong. And with this realization came the immediate solution. He had been caught in a sexual catch-22 all his life. His very yearning for feminine approval was what made women despise him.

Now, deep inside him, he could feel that something had changed. He honestly didn't give a fuck any more. For the first time ever, he knew that the key to his happiness lay not in what other people did to him, but in what he did to other people.

All he needed, in order to be happy, was to do what he wanted. It was obvious. He had to cast aside his fear of being judged or rejected, and pursue his own desires, regardless of what other people thought of him. If he succeeded, he would attract a certain amount of hatred, particularly from women, but it wouldn't matter. If he was properly in touch with his own mind, and his life revolved intelligently around his own needs, then even the deepest scorn from a woman wouldn't affect him. In fact, it would be a sign that he was succeeding.

At last, Josh knew what to do. He would put himself first. It was how he acted that mattered – not how other people judged him – and from now on, he would act with strength. He would take control of his own destiny.

13

There was only one flaw in Josh's plan. Lisa. She was the only person whose good opinion Josh felt he still needed.

When he returned to work the following week, Lisa waited until lunchtime, took him for a sandwich, then asked him what had really happened with Keri. Josh had only a few moments to decide what to say, and before even managing to open his mouth, he knew that his hesitation had exposed the mugging story as a fiction.

'What did Keri do to you?' asks Lisa, staring at him intently.

Before Josh has managed to wrestle a coherent and plausible response from his confused brain, Lisa puts her hand on his arm. 'I'm sorry,' she says. 'Keri can be a bitch. It was stupid to try and set you up together.'

Josh fights the desire to give Lisa an enormous hug and weep into her neck. He is so taken aback by her support for him – so surprised to hear an attack on Keri – that he feels a surge of love thump him in the chest. Suddenly, his emotions are utterly out of control as he realizes that Lisa's sympathy is stirring up all the misery he had been successfully holding at bay with the help of his video recorder.

His defences suddenly in tatters, he stands, mutters an apology, and charges for the toilet.

He returns a few minutes later, still adrenalized, but feeling less liable to sob without warning, and smiles tentatively at Lisa. 'I had to shit,' he says, without much conviction.

Lisa eats her sandwich in silence for a while, then asks him again what happened with Keri.

'I thought she was your friend,' says Josh.

'She is.'

'You just said she was a bitch.'

'*Can* be a bitch.'

'She's a good friend, though?'

'Good enough for me to know her bad side.'

'Which is?'

'Which is exactly what she did to you.'

'And what did she do to me?' he says, attempting to inflect the question with sarcastic bravado.

'You tell me,' she replies, instantly deflating Josh and making him want to cry again.

Josh stares out of the window. A curious urge to be honest flutters into his head, taking him by surprise. After a long silence, he mumbles, 'It's my fault because I know she didn't exactly declare love for me or anything . . . but I just thought that . . . you know . . . that me and her had found something. I was wrong, though.'

Lisa emits a breath through her nose: half way between a chuckle and a sigh.

'What?' says Josh. 'What does that mean?'

'Nothing. Just ... that's what she always does. That's what always happens.'

'What always happens?'

'Men fall for her quicker than she falls for them – so she dumps them for being over-keen.'

'What – you get ditched for liking her?'

'Yeah.'

'And if you didn't like her, she'd keep you?'

'Don't know. It never happens. You'd probably stand a better chance, though.'

'You're saying I should have played hard to get?'

Lisa laughs, then forces herself to stop by biting her lip.

'What? What's funny?' he says.

'Nothing.'

'What's so funny?'

'Sorry. Nothing. It's just a funny thought, that's all.'

'What?'

'You – playing hard to get with Keri.'

Lisa suddenly bursts out laughing again. Josh's head bows, and his forehead wrinkles into a frown.

Lisa takes a deep breath and purses her lips to eliminate the remainder of her smirk. 'Sorry,' she says, regretting the turn that the conversation has taken. Every time she discusses her friend, she always finds herself riding piggyback on the sexual superiority exuded by Keri to end up in easy man-squashing games.

She reaches out and takes Josh's hand. 'I'm sorry,' she repeats. 'Look – Keri's fucked up. She always hurts people, and doesn't even realize it. She doesn't understand what it feels like.'

'It's not just me then?'

'Josh!' she says. 'Haven't you heard what I said? You're fine. It's not you. It's her.'

'You're not just saying that?'

'Whatever she does, she makes other people feel small. She does it to me. She can't help it.'

Josh opens his mouth, feeling strangely anxious about a sentence which seems to be rolling towards the tip of his tongue. He doesn't know exactly what it is, but a flutter in the pit of his stomach tells him that he is on the verge of saying something that will change his life.

'I need another shit,' he says.

He stands and walks from the table, his heart pounding. He's not quite sure what it was that made him alter his course at the last moment, but he knows that he only narrowly avoided declaring his long-repressed love for Lisa.

Watching him walk away, Lisa feels a renewed sense of warmth towards Josh. Although it would horrify him to know it, Josh always aroused in her a desire to mother him. The more he showed off, the more she saw his desperation to have her approval. Now, she felt that she had seen a more insecure and unhappy Josh than ever before. With his defences down, Josh seemed more needy and vulnerable than ever.

With Guy, Lisa was never quite in control. Guy's mixture of reticence and self-sufficiency made Lisa fear that after all their years together, she had never quite got under his skin. They were interdependent in all sorts of practical ways, but emotionally she often feared that Guy held all the cards. There was no way of knowing what he really thought. Guy himself probably didn't even know what he really thought.

Alone at a table in the sandwich bar, waiting for Josh to return from the toilet, she suddenly understood why her affection for him was taking root so deeply. He was, in a sense, the perfect rebound from the boyfriend she still had. Josh displayed the very character traits that were missing in Guy. The more transparent and insecure Josh appeared, the more Lisa liked him. In lots of ways Josh was an idiot, but she was beginning to realize that her years with Guy had created new insecurities in her personality which had barely existed before she met him – insecurities which were unwittingly soothed by Josh.

The solidity of her relationship with Guy had somehow undermined her. They were so claustrophobically tied together that she had become half a person. Everything in her life was halved. Her friendships, her time, her opinions, her bed – she had nothing to herself.

Although no one else could see it, Guy dominated her. She was always the one making the noise, but it was only ever Guy steering their course as a couple. In his quiet, intransigent way, Guy never let anyone else take control. He was incapable of genuinely relinquishing anything to Lisa. They were almost becoming a parody of a middle-aged couple: Chatty Sociable Wife and The Silent Man Who Always Drives. They both colluded in presenting themselves to the world as a female-dominated couple while in fact, behind closed doors, she was being quietly, systematically stripped of her individuality.

With utter clarity, it hit Lisa that Guy weakened her – not deliberately – simply by the fact of having forced her into a position of humiliating reliance. The longer she stayed with him, the more she shrank as a person.

With Josh, by contrast, she felt powerful. Josh's first instinct was always to defer to her. He always seemed to assume that she was more experienced, better informed and wiser than him.

Josh respected her. He looked up to her. He was, perhaps, closer to loving her than her boyfriend of four and a half years.

As Josh returned to the table and sat down opposite her with a loud I-did-a-big'un sigh, Lisa sensed, with a twinge of excitement, that her life was now far more complicated than it had been two minutes before. Suddenly pain, trauma and disaster were hovering in the wings, waiting for their cue.

14

'Did you . . . ?'

'What?'

'Did you and Helen . . . ?'

'What?' says Graham, pretending not to understand the question.

'You know.'

'She's a nutcase, Guy.'

'I thought that was the point. You like mad women.'

'Who says I like mad women?'

'You.'

'I don't like mad women. I just like women.'

'Mad ones.'

'Sometimes. Not because they're mad. Just because they're women.'

'Anyway – did you . . . ?'

'Did I what?'

'Did you and Helen . . . ?'

Graham stares at Guy inquisitively – as if waiting for something. 'That's not a question,' he says. 'That's half a question.'

'Did you shag? Did you fuck?'

Graham wrinkles his face, thinking. 'She's your friend?' he says, eventually.

'Of course she is.'

'A good friend?'

'Yeah.'

'Then why did she act like that?'

'Like what?'

'Like she hates you.'

'Thanks, Graham. Nicely put. Very delicate. Making sure you don't hurt my feelings or anything.'

'She did, though. She was acting like she thinks you're a wanker.'

'That's just her.'

'It wasn't her. It was you. She was nice to me. Then she treated you like a wanker.'

'She's like that. She's . . . you know . . . complicated. She has moods and comes over all stroppy, then gets upset and apologizes and the whole thing goes round and round like that endlessly. I'm one of the only people who sticks by her.'

'You're sure she doesn't just think you're a bit of a cock?'

'You find this whole idea really funny, don't you?'

'What?'

'You're trying to get me to say that my friends hate me.'

'Well it is funny. I hate you.'

'Thanks.'

'Seriously,' says Graham. 'Tell me. She's a nutter . . .'

'Forget it.'

'Please. I'm interested.'

'You're not interested. If you were interested, you'd stop interrupting me every ten seconds to tell me I'm a cock.'

'You are a cock.'

Guy barks an exasperated laugh.

'You are. You're a cock,' repeats Graham.

'Graham–. . .'

'You cock.'

'Is this your idea of a conversation?'

'Yeah.'

'You're not going to tell me if you shagged her?'

'I might if you ask.'

'I have asked.'

'When?'

'Did you shag her? I'm asking you now.'

'You want to know if I shagged her?'

'Yes!'

Graham frowns and sinks deep in thought, as if trying to dredge up the answer from a distant corner of his memory. 'Errr . . . sort of,' he says.

'What do you mean, sort of?'

'Sort of, as in . . .' Graham pauses to search for the word. 'As in . . . no.'

'Aaaaaah! I knew it!' Guy slaps the table with glee. 'I knew it!'

'Thanks for the sympathy.'

'I knew you wouldn't!'

'She's clearly a bit . . . you know . . . repressed. Frigid.'

'Wrong!' chimes Guy.

'What?'

'Wrong!'

'What do you mean, "wrong!"?'

'She's not repressed. She's quite promiscuous.'

'She's promiscuous?'

'Yeah.'

'Really?'

'Yeah.'

'FUCK!' Graham stares at Guy, horrified by this piece of news. 'Why didn't you tell me? Fucking hell!'

'Tell you?'

'Yeah.'

'Why?'

''Cause . . . it would have . . . I would have . . . you know . . . I didn't have any idea. You didn't tell me she was *promiscuous*. I would have tried harder. I can't believe it! I gave up so quickly.'

'It's not about *giving up*. If she's not interested, she's not interested. Persistence isn't going to help. Clearly you're just not . . . attractive enough.'

'She's *promiscuous*? Christ! You'd never guess.'

'It's always a disaster, though. That's why I thought you and her might not be such a bad thing. She always sleeps with the biggest tossers, then gets shat on, and ends up in a spiral of increasing misery.'

'You wanted me to top up her misery?'

'I thought you might actually be nice to her.'

'I *was* nice to her.'

'But she didn't sleep with you. Which proves the whole thing.'

'What whole thing?'

'Her problem. She's only attracted to men who she knows will shit on her. She's got an S-bend complex.'

'So if I hadn't been nice to her, she might have shagged me.'

'Maybe. If you were nasty enough.'

'Fuck! Why didn't you tell me?'

'To be nasty?'

'Yeah.'

'She's my *friend*!'

'*I'm* your friend.'

Guy laughs, stands, and edges out from behind the table.

'I have needs!' shouts Graham, calling to Guy's retreating figure, as it wobbles toward the crowd around the bar. 'You should have told me, you cock.'

15

'You know what it is next week?' says Guy.

Lisa, wandering in and out of the bedroom, adding and removing various bits of clothing, eating a bowl of cereal, drinking a cup of tea and blow-drying her hair, seemingly all at once, ignores the question.

'Why don't you get up?' she says.

'Because I don't have to.'

'So? *I* have to.'

'You want me to get up out of guilt?'

'I can think of nicer ways to put it,' she says, leaving the room.

'OK,' he calls after her. 'I'll get up if you tell me what it is next week.'

'APRIL!' she shouts, from the kitchen.

'NO!'

'It is. Now get up,' says Lisa, suddenly appearing by the bed, and throwing aside the duvet. A fusty smell wafts out, and Guy sits up.

'It's also our fifth anniversary,' he says.

'Bollocks.'

'It is.'

'Guy – you're fantasizing. We're nowhere near five years.'

'Lisa – don't you remember? We first got together

when I came back late from my parents' house after my dad's fiftieth-birthday party. You were still up in your room having an essay crisis, and I saw your light on and sneaked up and rogered you.'

'So romantic.'

'You remember, though?'

'I remember the essay.'

'Very funny.'

'It was on Gertrude Stein and Sylvia Plath, but I never finished it.'

'Look – Mum rang yesterday and told me that Dad's turning fifty-five next week.'

'Really?'

'Yup.'

Lisa puts down her tea and frowns, staring at the carpet. 'Shit,' she says.

'What?'

'Five years. Fucking hell.'

'You sound really delighted.'

'Five years. Christ.'

'I think we should celebrate,' says Guy. 'Have a fifth-anniversary party.'

'Are you serious?'

'Course I am.'

'For God's sake, Guy. How can you be so tacky?'

'What's tacky about a fifth-anniversary party?'

'It's private. We're not married. We've just been seeing each other for a long time, that's all. It's nothing to show off about.'

'It's an achievement. We've stuck together.'

'Look – forget it. There's no way I'm parading our private . . . extended . . . tolerance of each other as some kind of . . . just forget it.'

'What's your problem?'

'FORGET IT!'

'What do you mean, extended tolerance?'

'Just . . . forget it. I'm not interested. We haven't got anything to brag about.'

Lisa stares at him icily, then marches from the room, already confused by the violence of her reaction. She doesn't quite understand why the idea rattles her so much. Perhaps it isn't so much the notion of the party as the realization of how long she has been with Guy. The fact that she has completed half a decade with a man she can feel herself beginning to turn against strikes her as a horrific waste of time.

It's not that she already wants to split up with him – she just doesn't particularly feel like being with him any more.

She cleans her teeth, loads up her work bag, puts on her coat, and hovers by the front door. She puts one hand on the latch, then turns and walks back to the bedroom. Guy is still sitting on the bed, in the same position as before. He looks up and stares at her, inquiringly.

She sees the confusion and worry on his face. He knows something is wrong. Lisa has begun the process of silently ushering their problems into the open. A truce has been broken.

'Look,' she says, 'we can have a party if you want. Not an anniversary party. Just a party. OK?'

Guy shrugs his assent.

Lisa puts her bag down and kisses Guy gently on his lips, which don't kiss her back. She turns and leaves for work, again feeling a flutter of excitement from knowing that she has dropped a ticking hand-grenade into her life.

Lisa didn't know why, or how, but this tiny little non-argument somehow confirmed for her that their relationship was over. From now on, it was just a matter of time. She could feel a level of resistance to Guy which had quietly but firmly taken root inside her. The only remaining question was how that resistance would manifest itself, and how quickly Guy would respond to its presence.

This thought added a layer of relief to Lisa's excitement. She had made the decision, but from now on, it was out of her hands. Without conscious effort, her changed attitude would naturally become apparent. That was all she had to do. Small gulfs and disagreements would slowly form, and it would be up to Guy to figure out why, and to do something about it.

There was no obligation on Lisa to march home one day and tell Guy that she was falling out of love with him. She just had to relax and wait for the earthquake to arrive. It was the kindest way of doing it. No bolt-from-the-blue declarations, no screaming matches, no sudden betrayals – just the gradual dissolution of affection.

16

Guy and Lisa's preparation for the party extended to one supermarket visit. They bought a few armfuls of wine, a crate or two of beer, a tower of plastic glasses, laid them out on the kitchen table, and felt ready for their guests.

Predictably, Helen was the first to arrive.

'What a surprise!' says Lisa, with transparent sarcasm, as she opens the door and kisses Helen once on each cheek.

'I hope I'm not the first,' says Helen.

'I think you might be.'

'Oh, no. I'm half an hour late. I thought that would be enough.'

'Don't worry. It's lovely to see you.'

'It's embarrassing being the first.'

'Don't worry.'

'God,' says Helen, gingerly peering inside, as if to check the lack of other guests.

'Are you coming in, then?' says Lisa, rather more brusquely than she intended.

'Yes. Sorry. Yes.'

The minute Helen enters the flat, Lisa notices Guy's face light up.

'Hi!' he says, trotting toward Helen, and enveloping her in a bear-hug.

'Ooooh!' says Helen, which strikes Lisa as an odd kind of greeting.

'I saw Graham the other day,' says Guy, dragging Helen down to a position hard up against him on the sofa.

'Oh, I'm so sorry about that evening,' says Helen. 'I was in such a funny mood.'

'Strange, that,' mutters Lisa, inaudibly.

'I behaved awfully. I felt so guilty about what I'd done to you that I think I might have ended up taking it out on Graham. It was such a disaster.'

'You poor thing,' says Lisa – a private joke aimed at Guy. Every time Guy is on the phone to Helen, Lisa waits for the first time he says 'You poor thing' then mouths 'Bingo!' Sometimes she even times it, and congratulates him if he holds out for more than two minutes.

Guy scowls discreetly at Lisa, then turns back to Helen. 'It doesn't matter. The whole thing was an awkward situation. I shouldn't have been late, and . . .'

'It wasn't *your* fault.'

'Well, I . . .'

'It was me. It was all me. I messed the whole thing up, and I actually liked Graham – or sort of liked him – I didn't fancy him or anything – but I acted like a total idiot and gave him the wrong impression, then I couldn't get out of it without making him think I'm a complete weirdo.'

'No!' says Lisa. 'He wouldn't have thought that.'

'Helen,' says Guy, 'you mustn't take the blame for everything. I spoke to Graham about it, and he just said you didn't . . . hit it off in the long run . . . but he's not pissed off. He doesn't think it was your fault.'

'Really?'

'Yeah. He had a nice evening. He thinks you're interesting.'

'Really?'

'Of course he does.'

Lisa, shaking her head, walks to the kitchen. Although she wasn't present at the conversation, she knows for sure that 'interesting' is *not* the word Graham would have used to describe Helen.

* * *

The party was Josh's first chance to try out his new sexual persona. He was on the pull, and whoever he chose would be helpless before the onslaught of his newfound confidence, charm and ruthlessness.

By the time he arrived, just after ten, the flat was half full. He was greeted rather coldly by Guy, who pointed out where the drinks were then immediately disappeared, leaving Josh to fend for himself without having been introduced to anyone. The only person he knew was Lisa, and she was deep in conversation with a gaggle of women, sharing a series of rather exclusive-seeming jokes. One of the women was Keri, which ruled out not just Lisa, but that entire room.

Josh wandered around the crowded flat for a while, walking purposefully in an attempt to give the impression that although he wasn't talking to anyone, he was on his way to talk to someone in another area of the party.

Everyone seemed to be in impenetrable conversational groups, except for one girl who was hovering in the hallway, alone, gulping rather recklessly at a glass of red wine, drinking with the intensity of someone using alcohol as a substitute for company. Josh checked her out and zeroed in.

'Hi, I'm Josh,' he says, at that moment wondering to himself if chat-up lines really did exist.

'Hi,' she says, with an unhappy-looking smile. 'Helen.'

'Do you know anyone else here?' says Josh.

'Most people,' she replies. 'I'm an old friend of Guy's.'

'Oh. Right,' says Josh, rather confused, since he was offering the question as an excuse for their mutual solitariness, with the assumption that she'd say 'no'. Her answer makes her sound rather . . . well, strange. What *is* she doing alone in the corridor gulping wine like medicine, if she knows lots of people?

What the hell, he thinks. Strange is good. Strange

and already-on-the-way-to-being-pissed at only ten o'clock is even better.

'Have we met before?' he says.

'Yes,' she replies, in an accusatory tone.

'Errr . . . I work with Lisa,' he says, fishing for the source of a vague, slowly emerging half-memory of Helen. 'At her office.'

'Oh,' says Helen.

'So I just know Lisa. I met Guy once before. But I don't really know him.'

'He invited you to dinner. I was there. At the end.'

'Right. Yeah. I knew I recognized you. I knew it. You're his . . . like . . . oldest friend.'

'One of.'

'He's nice.'

'Yeah.'

'Him and Lisa are . . . er . . . nice,' he says, his mind suddenly blank as to any possible subjects for conversation. He simply can't think of anything to say.

Helen nods at him, half smiling. He nods back.

As the silence begins to approach an embarrassing length, he opts for repetition. 'They're nice,' he says. 'I like them. Er . . . How long have they been together? Do you know?'

Helen shrugs and takes another gulp of wine. Silence descends again. This was like talking to a tree. A hostile tree.

On the point of giving up with her, Josh resolves

to grit his teeth and press on. After all, he's out to prove something. No sullen, self-absorbed woman is going to make *him* feel small. If she doesn't want to talk to him, it's not his problem; it's her problem. And he has to show her that.

With this in mind, he brushes off Helen's refusal to ask him any questions, and embarks on a lengthy monologue about his relationship with Lisa, and his job. Perhaps not exactly *his* job, but a job resembling it, with more authority, more excitement, higher wages and less photocopying.

* * *

By midnight the flat is crammed with people, all shouting over one another to get heard, causing the one lone dancer to turn up the stereo, causing the shouters to shout more, in turn resulting in extra volume from the stereo and more shouting.

Guy stands on a chair. He clangs two empty beer bottles together, and mimes a demonstration of spin bowling to the back of the room, which is eventually interpreted as a request to turn the music down.

The level of talk slowly dwindles to a few hecklers, who confusingly start yelling 'SPEECH!' at Guy, regardless of the fact that this is clearly his intention anyway, and they are the only people stopping him.

'Listen! Listen!' he says, before suddenly being stabbed by a moment of panic. He's not sure where Lisa is. He scours the room with his eyes, then spots her, leaning against a door-frame in the corner, beer bottle clutched to her chest, staring at him with what looks suspiciously like hatred. The scowl on her face confirms the very thing he had been afraid of, but now he has the attention of everyone in the room, it seems too late to back down. Equally, he can feel a perverse, barely conscious drive within him, pushing him to defy her in public.

'I know Lisa didn't want me to say anything . . . but . . . but seeing you all here . . . everyone I most . . . care about and hang out with and have known for ages . . . and you're all really great people . . . and seeing you all here, I just felt this big urge to share with you something that . . . I just felt that with everyone here this was the best time to just say . . . I mean to let you all know . . . It's not a big thing or anything . . . I mean I'm not trying to make anything massive out of it or anything . . . but I'm just very proud and grateful that we've managed to . . . that me and Lisa . . . this is our fifth anniversary.'

Huge cheers instantly fill the air, only slightly muted by the fact that every single person in the room had assumed he was about to announce their engagement.

The sheer noise of this response surges through Guy's body like a rush of alcohol. He steps from his chair to the floor, feeling weak with relief. He doesn't know why, but this public acceptance of his success with Lisa seems to represent a confirmation of something important. With everyone sharing in the happiness of the anniversary, he feels as if he has somehow diluted the painful claustrophobia of crossing the five-year barrier. Perhaps not just diluted, but transformed. Between the two of them, the experience seemed to have conjured up a distressing lack of joy.

He had been right about the party and about the speech. He had salvaged something positive in the face of Lisa's inexplicable destructiveness.

With everyone clapping and cheering, a small space opens up around Lisa. A couple of people kiss her on the cheek, and a corridor of carpet space through the crowd opens up between her and Guy. Lisa, it seems, has no option but to walk towards Guy and do something to turn his speech into a joint gesture. The whole room is silently insisting that she kisses him – as if his crap speech constitutes some great gift for which she should be swooning with gratitude.

She catches Guy's eye, and slowly walks towards him.

He can't quite read her expression. All he can tell is that she seems to be the only person in the room who isn't smiling. Her walk also seems strangely slow – less the blushing bride; more the boxer on his way to the ring.

She smiles thinly, and pecks him hard on the lips.

The hecklers start up again. 'SPEECH! SPEECH!'

'No. No. No way,' she says.

'SPEECH! SPEECH!'

'Forget it.'

'SPEECH! SPEECH! SPEECH! SPEECH! SPEECH! SPEECH! SPEECH! SPEECH!'

Lisa stares at Guy, her mouth screwed shut with rage. The noise swirls around them, with the chant from a pissed gang at the back of the room soon spreading to all the guests.

Guy has to put his lips right up against Lisa's ear to be heard. 'I'm sorry,' he says. 'You don't have to.'

She shoots him a scornful look. They both know she doesn't have a choice.

She raises a hand, and the chants turn into a cheer.

With her hand still raised, she steps up on to the vacated chair. This action is greeted with a louder cheer.

'OK!' she says. 'I'll make a speech.'

The noise dies down. Lisa stares around the room, feeling the strange perspective given by her vantage-point percolate into her mind as a form of power.

'I'll make a speech,' she repeats, rather oddly, into the silence of the room. Something in the way she says this makes the phrase sound like a threat. The silence deepens, her audience pricked by a tiny jolt of tension.

'Guy,' she says, turning to him and smiling. From above, he looks short and weak. His hair is already beginning to thin slightly on top. He smiles back at her through a long silence, his neck twisted to an awkward angle.

'Tell me,' she says, 'what are you playing at?'

Guy chuckles, embarrassed, scratches his nose, and glances at the room of guests.

'I'm interested,' she insists. 'Will you tell me exactly what the fuck you're playing at?'

Guy looks at her, his face whitening with shock. Everyone in the room is still.

'Did we not discuss this? Do you not remember what I said?'

'Look,' he says, 'can we . . .' he reaches up to take her hand, hoping to draw her outside.

She yanks her arm away sharply. 'Do you not FUCKING REMEMBER WHAT I SAID?'

'Please. Lisa.'

'I SAID IT WAS PRIVATE! I SAID IT HAD NOTH-ING TO DO WITH THIS PARTY!'

'No, *this* is private. Can we just –. . .'

'I thought you wanted to do everything publicly. Isn't this what you like? A show of public honesty.'

'Lisa . . .'

'What's wrong? Are you *embarrassed*? Do you not like it?'

Guy, realizing that he is trapped, turns on his heel, his head down, and leaves the room. In a moment of utter confusion he sees the toilet door ajar, steps through, and locks himself in. As a reflex, he pulls his trousers down and sits. His head in his hands, he stares at the floor, his mind whirring too fast for any actual thoughts to stick.

'OK,' says Lisa to the room of gawping faces. 'Show's over. Now you all know. We're middle-aged married farts, but at least we've still got the spunk to make each other miserable.'

With that she leaps from the chair and charges out of the room. The front door slams, and the packed flat is left in stunned silence.

Keri pushes through the stationary crowd, turns up the stereo to stop the party feeling like a wake, and follows Lisa out of the house.

Keri finds her sitting at a bus shelter a couple of minutes down the road. Seeing Keri approach, Lisa looks away, but doesn't move.

Keri sits next to her in silence, on a grey plastic tip-up seat.

'Are you OK?' she says, eventually.

Lisa doesn't answer.

'Cigarette?' says Keri, after a long silence, proffering a packet of Silk Cut.

'Fuck, yeah,' says Lisa, breaking into a spasmodic laugh.

Keri snaps open her lighter and flicks a flame to Lisa's lips. Lisa, who rarely smokes, sucks greedily, browning the cigarette paper around the tip. She inhales, coughs, laughs, coughs again, then smiles awkwardly at Keri.

'Oops,' she says.

Keri raises an eyebrow in sympathy as she lights

up. Lisa stares down the road at a car exercising a clumsy three-point turn in the middle distance.

Only as they are stamping out their cigarette ends on the pavement does Keri speak. 'Guy locked himself in the toilet,' she says.

Lisa snorts a laugh. 'If in doubt, crap. It's Guy's general philosophy of life.'

'That complex male psychology at work again.'

'Jesus!' says Lisa. 'What am I going to do?'

Keri waits a while before saying, 'Apologize.'

'Apologize? Me?'

Keri stares at Lisa, amazed that Lisa seems to think she's in the right. 'You're not going to apologize?'

'Why should I apologize? He . . . look . . . you don't even know what happened. He wanted an anniversary party – I said no – we settled on a normal party, with no mention of the anniversary. That was the whole point. That was the agreement. Then without even telling me he does that in front of everybody.'

'It was sweet. He only spoke for a minute.'

'He promised. It's a trust thing. If you can't trust someone . . .'

'Lisa – he gave you a little surprise speech. Get a bit of perspective.'

'A broken promise is a broken promise.'

'It was a romantic little surprise.'

'It was embarrassing.'

'OK – maybe you didn't like it – that's no reason to humiliate him in front of all his friends.'

'What?'

'You didn't have to humiliate him like that.'

'*What?*' Lisa stares at Keri, her jaw open. 'You . . .' She tails away, shaking her head.

'What?' says Keri, baffled by Lisa's apparent outrage.

'You're . . .' Again, Lisa tails away, as if speechless.

'What's wrong?' says Keri.

'*You're* telling *me* I shouldn't have humiliated him?'

Keri stares at Lisa, feeling a defensive anger rise slowly. 'Yes.'

'You can't see an irony, here?'

'No.'

'You honestly don't see why it seems a little strange that you are sitting there lecturing me about why I shouldn't humiliate someone?'

'I'm not lecturing you, Lisa.'

'Well shut the fuck up, then. You're in no position to tell me how to behave towards Guy.'

'I'm just trying to – . . .'

'Well don't, Keri. All right? You're the fucking kiss of death. You know you are. I do not need the woman who has spent her entire life prick-teasing, exploiting and humiliating every single man she has ever come into contact with telling *me* how to conduct my love life.'

'I'm not – . . .'

'You honestly don't have a fucking clue how much

harm you cause, Keri. All right? I have had an argument with my boyfriend, and between us, we can deal with it. *You*, on the other hand, have got a *big* problem. You shit on people. You really do. And if *you* come out of it OK, you don't even give a toss.'

Keri stands, breathing hard. Her arms rise up, then slap down against her sides with exasperation. 'You're unbelievable, Lisa! You are unbelievable! If you could see how you look . . .'

Lisa stands and eyeballs Keri, daring her to finish her sentence.

Keri holds her gaze. Slowly and levelly, she says, 'You . . . are such a child. You can't even see what you've just done. It doesn't register in your brain. You attack him, you attack me, you'll do anything to avoid looking at yourself and seeing what a selfish, immature little bitch you are.'

'Listen, Keri – . . .'

'No, *you* listen. Maybe some men are a bit upset that I don't want to immediately marry them after one unsatisfactory little poke, but that's their problem. I don't belong to them. I'm not breaking any commitments; I'm not lying to anyone; I'm just moving on until I find someone I actually *like*. What you are doing to Guy – *that* is humiliation.'

'You – . . .'

'Don't deny it, Lisa. He's stuck by you for five years – through a lot of crap – and I can see exactly what you're doing. I can see it. I'm not just talking about this evening, either.'

Lisa stares at Keri, her chest rising and falling with deep, heavy lungfuls of air. She wants to know what Keri knows. She wants to know what Keri thinks she can see. Somehow, before Guy had even picked up on it, Keri seemed to have figured out that Lisa was turning against him.

With the threat of her unspecified knowledge hanging in the air, Keri turns and walks back to the flat, probably, Lisa suspects, to talk to Guy.

On her way in, Keri bumps into Josh on his way out. He has his arm around a small, dark-haired girl who Keri vaguely remembers meeting once before. Josh grins at Keri, then turns so he is blocking the corridor and kisses the girl roughly on the lips.

Keri shudders with horror, and squeezes past.

At the top of the stairs, a tall guy in bizarrely ill-fitting clothes is rapping on the toilet door. 'Tell you what,' he's saying, 'if you come out I'll give you my Mon-opoly set, a pair of spare mudguards, and my collec-tion of wooden phones.'

'Fuck off,' says Guy from behind the door, his voice wobbly with reluctant laughter.

'All right, all right! And . . . a length of pipe.'

'Is he OK?' says Keri.

'He drives a hard bargain, I'll tell you that.'

Keri chuckles. 'You are . . . ?' she says.

'Graham. I'm Guy's mentor.'

'Have we met before?'

'I've seen you from afar. Lisa never introduces me to any of her glamorous friends.'

'Why not?'

'Embarrassment,' he says, with pride.

Keri laughs again. She feels giggly – her body tingling with an after-buzz of tension from the argument. All her senses feel heightened in a manner which, it fleetingly occurs to her, is rather similar to sexual arousal.

'Right,' she says, trying to rein in her laughter. Without quite knowing why, she even hits Graham on the chest, as a way of preparing a serious voice with which to address Guy. She takes a focused breath, then knocks on the toilet door.

'Guy?' she says. 'It's me. Why don't you come out?'

'I will if you get rid of Graham,' says an echoey voice from inside the toilet. 'He keeps trying to swap things.'

'They're gifts! I told you!' yells Graham.

'I'll take him to the kitchen,' says Keri. 'In one minute, it'll be all clear.'

'OK.'

'Do you want to talk?' she adds, after a moment's silence.

'Another time,' says Guy. 'I want to go for a walk.'

'OK,' says Keri. 'I'll see you soon.'

In the kitchen, Graham tells Keri that she did exactly the right thing, since he had been on the verge of offering his Silver Jubilee souvenir torch.

17

Helen wasn't sure why she didn't resist when, out of the blue, Josh lunged at her in the corridor. It was one of those strange moments in life when you have a fraction of a second to decide whether you are outraged and never want to see someone again, or whether you like it and want to initiate the procedure of getting them into bed.

Helen didn't like it, but she wasn't outraged, either. She really didn't care what happened either way. She hadn't warmed to Josh, and wouldn't have minded if he disappeared, but spending a little more time with him seemed, on balance, a less unpleasant proposition than remaining at the party.

The only reaction she could manage was indifference. Within seconds, it was clear that this failure to take a decision, which manifested itself as a cool but not actively resistant response to his kiss, had been interpreted as assent.

So – assent it was.

After the kiss, Josh's bearing seemed to change. Before, he had been nervously monologueing at her, bragging about his trivial-sounding job, visibly sweating with the effort of sustaining a one-sided conversation, but from the moment he realized that Helen might actually be on his side, he seemed to relax. He even asked her a few questions about her job. She explained to him about her charity, and the work they did in Israel, which held his attention for several full minutes, before he interrupted her to say he didn't know that Zionist charities existed, then got all flustered in case she interpreted his comment as anti-Semitic. Which, on some level, she did.

The fact that she didn't really like Josh made Helen, in a perverse way, warm to him. She felt in control. She knew exactly where she stood, with no risk of unwelcome emotions rising up to hurt or surprise her. She didn't need him or even want him. He couldn't do anything to hurt her. This was a vain, self-absorbed, and not particularly intelligent man. She could do whatever she wanted with him. The power was all hers.

She had something that he wanted. He had come up to her, without prompting, and gone to enormous, visibly painful lengths to impress her – to try and get from her the thing that she could as yet decide whether or not to hand over. He was implicitly begging her for favours, and this was the best reason for staying with him just a little while longer – even for staying with him beyond the end of the party, when the stakes would be raised. It would be fun: controlled, safe fun.

With a guy like this, she wasn't exposed. She had him dangling on a string and she could make him dance, or she could snip.

So when Josh offers to call for a cab – one cab – she shrugs a yes. With the driver waiting to set off, he asks her where she lives.

'Camden,' she says.

'Clapham,' Josh replies.

They stare at each other, then she shrugs again, this time meaning, 'OK – Camden's closer.'

The second they are through Helen's front door, he envelops her in his arms and kisses her on her mouth and cheeks. It takes some effort for her to wriggle free.

'Shhh,' she says. 'Wait.' She gestures him to stay still, then tiptoes down the corridor a few steps, cocks her head, and tiptoes back.

'My flatmate's in the kitchen,' she whispers.

'Where's your bedroom?' he says, anxiously.

She looks at him, pauses, then indicates the way.

Helen closes the bedroom door behind them, lowering the handle so it doesn't click. Meanwhile, Josh draws the curtains, shutting out the glare from a nearby streetlight and slipping the room into darkness. Then Josh's arms are again wrapped around her, kissing her with a desperation that seems to be mimicking passion.

Still kissing her, he unbuttons her blouse and drops

it on the floor. He fumbles with her bra and drops that on the floor, too. Bending over, he kisses her breasts, sucking one after the other, then kneels in front of her. Helen watches, feeling more like a spectator than a participant, while he wrestles with the button fly of her jeans.

In one movement, he pulls down her trousers and knickers, but they jam round her ankles. He struggles with her shoes, pulls them off, then tugs her trouser legs over her feet. He then stands up and kisses her again, in a tight hug, the buttons of his clothes rubbing painfully against her naked flesh.

She glimpses a look of intense seriousness on his face as he steps back and begins to tear off his clothes. She lifts each foot, one after the other, and removes her socks, which Josh hasn't bothered with, all the while sensing something strange in the haste with which Josh is undressing. She notices that he is not even slightly aroused.

Naked, he hugs her again, this time more gently: with one hand around her back, and one hand under her bum. He holds her still, and she begins to relax, then suddenly he has lifted her off her feet and she is lying next to him on her bed.

Josh's strange urgency returns as he kisses her mouth, face and neck. His kisses are hard and fast, leaving her no room to kiss him back. All the while, Josh writhes on top of her, rubbing his swelling penis against her belly and legs.

As he plants one knee between hers, then another, a bolt of fear punches her in the stomach. This man hates her. She dislikes him, but he hates her. This isn't sex. This is something else.

'Wait,' she says. 'Slow down.'

Josh responds by pinning her arms against the mattress.

'Stop!' she says. 'Please. Slow down.'

Helen writhes, trying to push Josh away with her knees, while he squirms between her legs, jabbing with his penis, almost penetrating her. Her mind feels at once lucid and numb, racing through calculations of how to fight him off, while at the same time wondering, almost calmly, why she isn't screaming. Fixated, against logic, on the presence of her flatmate as a reason for not making any noise, she can't scream. She isn't screaming.

Then, momentarily, Josh's grip slackens on one of her forearms. She twists her hand around his wrist in a small circle, a movement she was taught years ago and thought she had forgotten. Her arm comes free. She clamps her fingers on his Adam's apple and squeezes with all her might. His face reddens, and she feels his neck muscles spasm under her fingertips. He stares at her, eyes bulging, looking surprised – almost offended – by her violence.

He tries to push her hand away, but this puts him off balance and she shoves him aside, sliding free and leaping out of bed in one movement. She stands, up against the wall, flinching as he falls to his knees on the far side of the room, coughing. A dirty jumper is on the floor by her feet. She grabs it and dives inside, stooping slightly and pulling at its hem to be more fully covered by the wool. She glances around the room for another item of clothing, but doesn't dare take her eyes off Josh or move one step in his direction. Nothing else is within reach.

Now on all fours, catching his breath, Josh gags, sounding as if he is about to vomit. When his chest stops heaving, he stands and stares at her, rubbing his throat with one hand, covering his genitals with the other. She stares back, blinking, at the same time feeling as though she is watching herself look at him – observing from above, seeing the whole thing happen to someone other than her, to a not-Helen whose fate seems curiously unimportant.

With precise, almost robotic movements, Josh dresses. She can't understand why he isn't hurrying. At the door he turns to her, opens his mouth to say something, then changes his mind. Seeming momentarily reluctant to leave, he shuffles into the corridor and pauses, glancing back one last time, before disappearing from view.

The door swings shut behind him.

The moment she is alone, her calmness vanishes. She notices that her hands are trembling. The sight, then the sensation, of this inability to hold herself still yanks sharply at her insides, like a plummet down a lift shaft. A wave of sobs suddenly convulses her body.

She slumps to the floor and curls up tightly, her one conscious thought focused on staying quiet enough to keep her flatmate out of the room.

Suddenly cold, she pulls at a corner of duvet, wrapping herself into a cocoon. Her body now tingling with panic, she closes her eyes, crushingly tired, yet sensing an unshakeable wakefulness. Like trying to sleep a bad drug out of your system, she knows that any attempt to slip out of consciousness is futile, and will only make her feel worse, but there is nothing else she can do – nothing that won't make her feel worse. This fizz of panic will rule her for many hours more, maybe even days, or weeks, or longer. This evening, this hour, her life has changed.

18

As this is happening, the party at Guy and Lisa's begins to tail away. First Guy returns from his walk, prompting an exodus of the embarrassed, then Lisa arrives, causing even the most thick-skinned to head for the front door. Keri and Graham jointly decide to stay and help with the clearing-up, their main intention being to stave off any potential homicides.

Keri and Graham chat noisily, passing between each other a series of increasingly desperate attempts to keep silence at bay, while Lisa and Guy stalk around the flat, neither catching the other's eye. When they have filled several bin-liners with bottles, cans and ash, returning the flat to something resembling its normal state, Keri offers to hoover.

Lisa turns to Graham, as the only apparently neutral party in the room, and says, 'No. You'd better go.'

'OK,' he replies, straining to go along with the pretence that he was the one who made the offer.

'Thanks for your help,' says Lisa, again only to Graham.

'No problem,' he says, at that moment accidentally catching Keri's eye and smirking.

Deciding he can't take the tension any more, Graham heads for the door, pecking Lisa on the cheek and patting Guy's arm on the way out.

'See you soon,' he says.

Keri follows immediately behind him, ignored by Lisa, kissed warmly by Guy.

In the front garden of Guy and Lisa's house – which isn't in fact a garden at all, but an area of concrete the size of a ping-pong table scattered with rubbish bags – Graham and Keri grimace at one another. They both want to scream with relief at being out of the flat, but know they are within earshot.

Graham puts his fist in his mouth and bites, knocking his knees together in pantomime agony. Keri, not wanting to make any noise, hits him as a substitute for laughter.

They haven't called a cab, and it is now almost one-thirty, so they walk towards the nearest main road to see what they can find. Only when they have reached the end of the street do they feel they can talk aloud.

'Ooohhhh!' says Graham.

'God!' replies Keri.

'Aahhh!'

'Eurrgh!'

'Oooofff!'

'That,' says Keri, 'was a *bad* evening.'

'So bad. It was actually painful. Physically.'

'You're right. I think I'm aching. I've got cramp.'

'No one,' he says, 'not even the Carpenters, has ever made an album as bad as that evening.'

'You reckon?'

'Definitely. It's a well-known fact.'

'What about Genesis?'

'Errr . . . OK . . . Maybe Genesis.'

'Robson and Jerome?'

'And Robson and Jerome.'

'Whitesnake?'

'And Whitesnake.'

'All Hawaiian music ever recorded?'

'All right, all right – so there are a lot of albums as bad as that evening, but they are all very bad albums,' he says. 'And you've got to admit it was a pretty good analogy.'

Keri laughs. 'You're right. Thanks for helping me get my head round things.'

'Any time. And you forgot Klaus Wunderlicht's organ renditions of favourite Beatles tunes.'

'You're not into organ renditions of favourite tunes? I love those.'

'Sometimes,' he says. 'If I'm in the right mood. If I've lent out all my Coldstream Guards Marching Band Plays Popular TV Themes albums, I might put on a few organ renditions.'

'CAB! CAB!' she shouts, suddenly jumping into the street and waving to a taxi with both hands as if the driver was in a distant ship on the horizon, rather than a passing car.

The taxi draws to a halt, with the driver shaking his head at Keri, and the pair of them get in. 'You're good at hailing cabs,' says Graham.

'Sorry,' she chuckles. 'Got a bit carried away.'

'Don't apologize,' he says, 'It's cool. I wish I had the . . . er . . . shamelessness to do it like that.'

She laughs.

'Where to?' says the driver.

'Where do you live?' says Keri.

'Ummm . . . just up the road. I can walk, actually.'

Keri laughs again. 'What are you doing in the cab, then?'

'Don't know. I was just keeping you company.'

'Do you want a lift?'

'Errr . . . yeah. Why not?'

He leans forward and gives his address to the driver, who immediately executes a perfect U-turn.

'Where do you live?' says Graham.

'Bethnal Green.'

'Bethnal Green?'

'Yeah.'

'Bethnal Green?'

'Yes!'

'I didn't know people lived in Bethnal Green. I thought it was just a place.'

'It is a place. It's a place with people.'

'I suppose it would be.'

'I like it there. And it's quick to work.'

'Right. You work in Mile End or something?'

'The City.'

'Right. OK. Which city?'

'You know what?' she says.

'What?'

'For every funny thing you say, you'll say something else that's just shit.'

'Really?'

'Yeah. That one was . . . it was stupid.'

'You're right. You're right. The whole thing's a bit hit and miss.'

'It's OK, though,' she says. 'It's worth it for the funny ones.'

'I'm pleased you think so. Most people don't.'

'Really?'

'It's hard to tell, but I think most people take me for a twat.'

'Oh, nooooo,' says Keri, with exaggerated sympathy.

'Sad but true,' he says, mournfully. 'I'm intensely unpopular.'

'Rubbish.'

'Oh, yes,' he says. 'I'm vastly hated.'

'I don't hate you,' she says.

'You're a weirdo, then. You're a genetic freak. You should get yourself seen to before it . . . ruptures your . . . face.'

Keri laughs again – a bubbling, easy, generous sound that makes Graham almost want to cry with gratitude for the existence of females.

The cab draws to a halt, and Graham reluctantly steps out. He then realizes that this means he has missed his opportunity to kiss her goodbye, so he gets back into the cab, kisses her on the cheek, and gets out again.

He turns, fishes inside his pocket and mimes at her to open her window. She slides it down, and he hands her a fiver, which she refuses to take. 'Don't worry,' she says.

He drops the money into the cab and says, 'Ooops!'

She shakes her head, plucking the money from next to her feet.

'Do you . . . want to . . . go for a coffee . . . some time?' he says.

'Yeah. Sure.'

'Shall I . . . ring you . . . ?'

'YES!' says the cabbie, sharply. 'Ring her! 'Cause now she's going.'

'Get my number off Guy,' she says. 'If he hasn't killed himself. If he has killed himself, get it off Lisa.'

'Bethnal Green?' says the cabbie.

'Please,' says Keri.

'What if they've killed each other?' says Graham.

'Then we'll never meet again,' she replies, with a pout, as the cab pulls away.

Graham stands on the kerb, watching Keri go. He can see her sitting sideways on her seat, watching him in return out of the back window.

As the cab draws round a corner and out of sight,

Graham ponders his chances. Well, he thinks, if I had plastic surgery, did body-building, spent my time finding out what clothes to wear, then somehow acquired the money to buy them, and at the same time learnt not to act like a twat, then maybe I'd stand a chance with her.

As it was, just having her as a friend – as someone he could take for a coffee – seemed like more of a sexual achievement than anything he had managed in the previous two years. He was proud to be in the position where he might be able to get her as a mate, and he felt honoured that she actually seemed to like him. He was a lucky man. And she – she was the perfect woman.

19

Adjacent in bed, the silence between Guy and Lisa is thick and stifling. They each feel it is the other's responsibility to initiate the inevitable round of apologies, but with both bedside lights off and the room in darkness, a stalemate settles in place. They haven't exchanged a single word since their argument.

They can hear one another's breathing, though, and both know that the other is awake.

Lisa, her face turned to the wall, quietly informs Guy that next week she is likely to be away, filming outside London.

'OK,' he replies. 'It might be for the best.'

'Mmm,' she says.

An hour passes, in silence, before Lisa and Guy drift, side by side, into sleep.

The following morning, Guy doesn't open his eyes until he has heard Lisa leave the house.

20

If the doorbell rings, and no one is expected, it's never good news. Someone you don't know will be offering something you don't want or demanding something you don't have. For this reason, and because the hallowed *Seinfeld/Sanders* hour is about to begin on TV, Guy almost doesn't answer. His curiosity gets the better of him, however, and he can't quite bring himself to ignore a persistently buzzing entryphone.

'Yeah?' he says, suspiciously.

The muffled sound of Keri's voice is completely unexpected. Guy can't quite make out what she is saying, so he buzzes her in.

She enters the flat clutching a bottle of whisky, and looks around the living room with a disappointed air.

'Lisa's away,' Guy says. 'Didn't you know?'

'Where?'

'Ipswich. She's filming the bathroom of a famous snooker-player.'

'What for?'

'Some documentary. Celebrity bathrooms. This guy's got a yellow, green, brown, blue, pink and black bathroom. With a green floor.'

'Oh. Right.'

'And he's turned his 1991 Embassy Matchplay runner-up medal into a tap. Lisa's filming it.'

'Right . . . I . . .' Keri sits on the floor, plonking the bottle of whisky on to the carpet in front of her, seemingly lost for words.

'We've got chairs . . .' says Guy, sitting himself on the sofa.

Keri smiles at him, but ignores his comment. 'I . . . came to see if you were all right. You and Lisa.'

Guy shrugs.

'Did Lisa tell you that we . . . er . . .'

'What?' says Guy.

'We had a bit of an argument. Just after she had a go at you. It was stupid, really. I wanted to . . . you know . . . apologize.'

'To Lisa?'

'Yeah.'

'Well she's not here. You'll have to apologize to me instead.'

Keri frowns at him, offended.

'Joke. I'm joking.'

'Oh,' says Keri, not quite understanding what Guy is on about.

After a while, Guy slaps his thighs and stands. 'Right!' he says, loudly. 'We'd better make a start on that whisky.'

Keri looks up at him and nods. Guy leaves the room to fetch a couple of glasses and calls from inside the kitchen, 'You don't want ice, do you?'

'Please.'

'You *do* want ice?'

'Yeah.'

'You're not supposed to have ice with whisky,' he says, poking his head round the door-frame.

'Says who?'

'Anyone who knows anything about whisky.'

'Well I know nothing about whisky,' she says, 'so I'll have ice.'

'Fuck it,' says Guy. 'I'll have some, too. It tastes better.'

He returns with a couple of ice-filled glasses, places them on the floor in front of Keri, and breaks the seal on the whisky. 'Listen,' he says, holding one hand up in the air and cocking his head slightly on one side. He pours a shot, the bottle producing a series of perfect glugs as the liquid passes through the neck, each one pitched a fraction lower than the one before.

'Ahhh!' he says. 'A fresh bottle of whisky makes the most beautiful sound in the world.'

'*That* was the most beautiful sound in the world?' says Keri.

'Within reason.'

'You haven't heard much music, then?'

Guy laughs, then shrugs. He slumps on to the sofa, and the pair of them sit in silence for a while, sipping their drinks, not quite catching one another's eye.

Eventually, Guy asks Keri what her argument with Lisa was about. She takes a long time to answer – so long that he even thinks she might be ignoring the question – before looking at him squarely and saying, 'You.'

Guy swallows, and an involuntary smile peels up the corners of his mouth. 'Right,' he says. 'That's my favourite subject.'

Keri looks at him sternly, refusing to acknowledge his attempt to lighten the tone. Guy's smile seeps from his face. 'What was the argument?' he says.

His question hangs in the air for a while, before Keri takes a long sigh. 'She's my oldest friend, Guy. You know I'm completely loyal to her. And I came here to apologize to her.'

'Yes . . .' Registering her evasions, Guy's face now begins to purse with tension.

'I just . . .'

'What?'

'I told her that I thought she'd shat on you.'

'Oh, right,' says Guy, the smile reappearing around the corners of his mouth. Something strikes him as slightly transgressive in this strange testimony of support. Although Keri was by now a mutual friend of both Guy and Lisa, nothing could ever dissolve the fact that she was Lisa's friend first. For Keri to express this unexpected loyalty to Guy, overriding her older loyalties to Lisa, felt like the breach of a previously impenetrable barrier.

Again, silence fills the room, before Guy asks, 'What did she say?'

Keri half smiles. 'She disagreed.'

Guy laughs. 'I suppose she would.'

They look at one another, both fleetingly lost in private recollections of Lisa's fierce temper.

'It's funny, isn't it?' he says.

'What?'

'Us. Us and Lisa.'

'What about us and Lisa?' says Keri.

'I don't know,' says Guy, backing off from what he was thinking, unsure quite what he was aiming at.

Keri, however, thinks she knows what he means. Keri and Guy love Lisa in the same way, and part of this is to dislike her in the same way. They both secretly think they understand her better than she understands herself – and recognize in each other an ally who has suffered Lisa's rages.

Keri smiles at Guy, feeling a glow of affection for him – even sensing that as Lisa's oldest friend, she shares a degree of responsibility for the way in which he has been let down. With an odd stab of guilt, she realizes that she feels a closeness and loyalty to Guy which is stronger than anything she feels for Lisa.

'Does she . . . ?' he says.

'What?'

'Can I ask you a stupid question?'

'Yes.'

'You'll give me an honest answer?'

'I'll try.'

'You promise?'

'Yes,' says Keri, anxiously – dreading what he is about to ask.

Guy tops up their glasses with two generous slugs of whisky. 'Do you think . . .', he says, '. . . do you think Lisa loves me?'

'Guy – you can't ask me that.'

'You said you'd answer.'

'Look – I'm far too involved as it is.'

'Because I don't think she does,' he says, suddenly – almost interrupting her. 'I don't think she ever has done. I don't think she's capable of it.'

Keri stares at him, stunned. She concentrates on trying not to show a reaction, since as soon as he said it, she could feel herself knowing that he was right. A moment of panic hits her when Guy's breathing becomes irregular and his face begins to twitch, as if on the verge of tears.

'Or maybe she did,' he says, 'a while ago. But she doesn't any more.'

He stands, gasps noisily – as if to regain control of his facial muscles – then slumps down on to the floor next to her, lying on his back, staring at the ceiling. She watches him, unable to think of anything to say.

Then he sits up, glugs down his whisky in one go, and lies flat on his back again. He looks at Keri. She smiles, picks up her glass, and glugs her whisky down in one. He watches her, looking briefly content, before misery again creeps across his features.

Keri shifts her position, and places a hand on his

forehead, pushing Guy's hair away from his eyes. 'Don't . . .' she says.

'What?'

'I don't know. Just . . . don't be . . . sad.'

He chuckles. 'I might try that,' he says.

'I know you *are*,' she says, 'but don't be.'

He looks at her, and it dawns on him that without either of them saying so, they are now discussing the fact that his relationship with Lisa is over. This realization dawns with a strange lack of emotional force. All he feels is a breath of relief sweeping through him. In a sense, the agony is over. His conscious mind has finally caught up with what he has known for several days: that there is nothing left between him and Lisa except resentment.

He sits up, and sloshes two large shots into the whisky glasses. He raises his drink, and holds it still at shoulder level. Keri lifts her glass, and chinks it against his. He tosses his head back and necks his whisky in one. As the drink burns down through his throat, a new thought pops into his head. He is now – suddenly – in all but the most literal sense – single.

As he puts his glass back on to the carpet, Keri swallows her shot of whisky, also in one gulp. She coughs, and her hand rises to her neck. Her long, slender, beautiful neck.

'You drunk? he says.

'Getting there,' she replies, with half a smile. 'You?'

'Almost.'

'Are you depressed?' she says.

'Getting there.'

Keri chuckles.

'You?' he says. 'You depressed?'

She shrugs. 'Not . . . depressed,' she says, ambiguously – as if a better, but similar word is eluding her.

He pours two more shots from the now half-empty whisky bottle, and downs his immediately. Keri looks at him askance, frowning slightly, then raises her glass and drinks it down in three slow swallows.

'Christ!' she says, a burst of alcohol exploding into her bloodstream. She thumps her glass down and topples sideways on to the floor. Allowing her arms to fall by her side, she rolls herself flat on to her back, and lies there, hair splayed around her on the carpet like a halo.

Guy smiles at her, but she doesn't look at him. Her eyes are shut.

He puts his hand on her belly. Her eyes remain shut.

He moves his hand along and down a fraction. Through her thin cotton trousers, he can feel the bulge of her hip bone. He looks at her face. Her eyes seem to close a fraction tighter.

Guy moves his hand lower still, into a slight indentation below the bone, then up again as her muscle rises, then down and sideways, off the firmness of her thigh, and into the warm softness between her legs.

He feels the slight spring of her pubic hair, then, lower, an intense glow of heat.

Her eyes still closed, she rocks her hips, and closes her legs tightly around his hand. He doesn't move, feeling her warmth spread into his fingers.

His pulse accelerates, and with a surge of adrenalin numbing his brain, he leans forward and kisses Keri, softly and slowly on the lips. He feels as if he can hear as well as taste and feel their kiss. A slightly blurred drunkenness is pressing at the sides of his brain, yet he also feels utterly awake and alive.

His skin tingles as he pulls away from her mouth and rubs his cheek against hers, marvelling at the softness of female skin, inhaling the magical secret smell of her neck. Her hand then reaches round to the back of his head, stroking him through his hair, and she pulls him back to her lips, into a wet, lingering kiss.

Slowly, kissing all the while, they remove one another's clothes, one item at a time, in alternation. Barely noticing what is happening, they shed layer after layer, gradually approaching nakedness.

The last item to go, with Guy lying on his back, is his socks. Keri then places one hand on his chest, and straddles him. He feels her wetness on the base of his penis, which is pressed flat against his belly. He moans, as she rubs against him.

She then raises herself, lifts his erection with one hand, and places his tip against her lips. Millimetre by millimetre, she slides back down, and Guy disappears into the hot, slow, universe-eradicating, soul-massaging sensation of slipping deeper and deeper and deeper inside Keri.

For a second he opens his eyes, just to give himself something to remember. Keri – beautiful, stunning Keri – is on top of him, her eyes shut, her features spread with private bliss.

Click.

He closes his eyes again, not wanting her to open hers and see him watching.

He places his hands on her buttocks as she allows her weight to fall forwards. Her warm skin rubs against his chest. His hands rise up, and his fingers grip tighter and tighter as she rocks subtly backwards and forwards, barely moving her body, nudging them in slow shunts to the cliff edge of orgasm.

Afterwards, back down at sea level, sensation gradually returns to their two brains, bringing guilt, horror and fear. As they lie there, tingling with the retreat of mental numbness, they each feel briefly alone. When they turn and spot the terror in one another's face, they both suddenly burst into nervous laughter.

'God!' says Keri. 'What was that?'

'I don't know.'

'Did that just happen?'

'I think so,' he says. 'There's a fair amount of evidence.' With his eyes, he directs her gaze to her own naked body, and to the clothes strewn around the room.

'Christ!' she says. 'I think it did. We just . . .'

They both laugh again.

'Well that's satisfied my curiosity, at least,' he says, making her laughter rise with half-genuine outrage.

'I can't believe we did that,' she says. 'I can't believe it. That was . . . that was . . . *such* a bad idea.'

Guy looks at her. 'A good bad idea,' he says.

She looks back, levelly, then allows the corners of her mouth to turn up. 'A good bad idea,' she concedes. 'But a good bad idea never to be repeated. Ever.'

'I know,' he says. 'It was an accident. An accidental collision of reproductive organs.'

'This is . . . this is . . . if she finds out . . .'

'She won't.'

'If she does . . .'

'She won't. I promise,' he says. 'I'm not ready to die.'

'*I'm* not ready to die.'

'She'd kill us,' he says. 'She would kill us.'

'But she won't. Because she won't find out.'

'Exactly,' he says.

'You promise?'

'Promise.'

'You don't have one of those . . . couple honesty-type things?'

'No . . . yes . . . whatever. I'm not telling. I'm really not telling.'

21

Within seconds of glimpsing Guy's face, Lisa knows that something's wrong. Or rather, something *is* wrong – their relationship has fallen apart, and Guy knows it – yet he is acting as if nothing is wrong. Which means that something *else* is wrong.

Something has happened. He's trying to hide something.

'So?' she says.

'What?'

'What's up?' she says.

'Nothing. How was your trip?'

'OK. The crew were wankers. The snooker player was a git. Geoff was being a tosser.'

'Sounds good.'

'What about you?' she says.

'Fine.'

'What did you do?'

'Nothing. Just work.'

'Good?'

'All right.'

'D'you get much done?'

'A bit. I did some constructive deleting.'

'Progress?'

'In a backwards kind of way, yeah.'

Guy has already picked up on Lisa's cagey suspiciousness. She normally doesn't ask what he's been up to, and *never* questions him on his Ph.D. He can't tell, however, whether she suspects what he has done, or is simply behaving strangely as a reaction to their argument – which they have still not discussed.

'Nothing happened, then?' she says.

'Like what?'

'I don't know. I'm just asking what you did.'

'I told you.'

'Good.'

'What's wrong?' he says. 'You're acting all weird.'

'Me?'

'Yeah.'

'It's you,' she says. 'You're acting weird.'

'I'm not. You are.'

'Look,' she says, 'if I'm acting weird, it's a reaction to you acting weird. When I walked in, I felt fine; now I feel weird. It's you.'

He stares at her, a strange, sickening emotion jostling his insides, shoving his unshakeable affection for Lisa up against an overwhelming desire to get her out of his life. A long silence persists between them, both feeling this same contradictory pull, each suspecting that it is mutual. They search one another's faces, approaching a moment of honesty, then Guy looks away.

'I've got some food on,' he says.

'Good. Great.'

167

'It's just a veggie sauce.'

'Brilliant.'

'D'you want rice or pasta?'

'Pasta,' she says.

'You don't want rice?'

'OK. Rice.'

'No. Pasta's fine,' he says.

'I don't mind.'

'Whatever you want. We'll have pasta.'

'I don't *want* pasta. I just said I don't mind. We can have what you want,' she snaps.

'I don't mind. So we'll have what you asked for.'

'Don't act like it's a big sacrifice, Guy. Just cook whatever you want.'

'All right,' he says. 'I will.'

'Good.'

'We'll have rice,' he says.

'Fine.'

'Good.'

Half-way through the meal, eaten in near silence, Lisa mutters, 'Sorry about the party. I was a bit . . . you know . . . out of it.'

'It's OK,' he replies, without looking up. 'Me too.'

They carry on eating.

In bed that night they have strange, edgy sex. They are both more emphatic and demanding than usual – their customary lazy familiarity nudged aside by a hint of roughness – and they come at the same moment, with an explosive intensity neither has felt for months.

22

With Lisa away filming, Josh was pleased to have a few days alone at the office to gather his thoughts.

Ever since his visit to Helen's flat, he'd been feeling strangely weightless – his mind in suspended animation. Whenever he tried to think about what he'd done, or even simply to remember the sequence of events, he confronted a blockage in his brain. Something prevented him from looking inside himself. He knew what had happened, and it shocked him, but his shock was intellectual, not emotional. He didn't actually *feel* anything.

Occasionally the word 'rape' sneaked into his head, then promptly disappeared. He didn't even need to banish it consciously. The idea simply passed through without registering.

Floating inside his oddly peaceful, conscience-free bubble, only one thing troubled him. Beyond a soft awareness of the gulf between what he knew he ought to be feeling and the minimal emotional response he had been able to conjure up, he vaguely sensed that worse was to come. The bubble would burst. He would land somewhere hard.

*

When Lisa returned to work, she noticed that Josh was less chatty than usual, but suspected this was largely embarrassment in the wake of her behaviour at the party. She assumed his silence was out of tact, stemming from a reluctance to probe into her problems, and she felt fleetingly grateful for this courtesy even though it was the precise opposite of what she actually wanted.

Lisa was desperate for him to ask about what had happened, because without being questioned she couldn't spontaneously start explaining herself, and without an explanation he would inevitably leap to unflattering conclusions. Anyone who didn't know the background of what Guy had done was bound to take his side.

As the day wore on, Lisa became increasingly needled by a desire to justify herself to Josh. The less he said, the more she feared he had judged her harshly. His muted behaviour fuelled her paranoia, and she soon felt not only embarrassed, but angry – convinced that his changed behaviour was because he now thought less of her. He had seen her at her worst and he would never forget it. Like everyone else, he had judged her, and judged her unfairly.

As always, the world's sympathy was being directed elsewhere. While other people were being comforted and listened to and cared for, no one even wanted to hear Lisa's side of the story. For every mistake she made, she was punished. Even Josh had refused to give her the benefit of the doubt.

Although she had barely done anything wrong, her brief explosion of temper at the party had been silently filed away as evidence against her, and the world had moved on without listening to Lisa's version of events. Another black mark. Another little humiliation in her life. And she just had to swallow it. She had to pretend that she, too, had moved on, then smile and chat through the disapproval, and work her way back to where she was before.

It was all, always, work.

Lisa felt that at birth, you were assigned a gradient. For someone like Keri, your life is lived on a downhill slope. There are maybe a few bumps and pot-holes, but you always have the momentum to coast through. You never even know the effort other people have to make to get anywhere. Lisa, by contrast, was always working against an incline. Constantly pedalling uphill, every inch of ground earned, Lisa never got anything for free. Everything was an effort.

And now, after twenty-six years, she deserved a rest. Soon, she would reach the crest of the hill. It had to happen soon. If she carried on, gritting her teeth, swallowing her little humiliations, not complaining, she'd eventually be rewarded. Life could only be unfair for so long. At some point, the luck would begin to balance out.

23

'Keri?'

'Yeah.'

'Hi. It's me,' says Lisa.

'Oh. Hi.'

'Hi.'

'Yeah. Hi,' says Keri. 'How was the . . . er . . . trip?'

'Fine. OK. Bit shit, really. You know . . .'

'Yeah. Yeah.'

'You?'

'Me?' says Keri. 'Yeah. Fine. I'm fine. Just . . .'

'What?'

'Working. You know.'

'D'you want to meet up?' says Lisa. 'After work. For some food.'

'Food? Today?'

'Yeah.'

'After work?'

'Yeah,' says Lisa.

'Er . . . OK. Great.'

'OK.'

'Great.'

'Fine.'

*

Meeting outside a small Italian restaurant in the cheaper porn-side-of-Wardour-Street half of Soho, Lisa gave Keri a hug.

Keri, who was usually greeted by Lisa with a peck on the cheek, interpreted this as an apology. Lisa wasn't a big apologizer, and on the scale of things this seemed like a reasonably heartfelt one, so Keri applied a little squeeze to let her know that it had been accepted, and that Keri apologized in return.

Despite this little moment of tactile togetherness, the atmosphere over dinner was tense. Keri kept telling herself that Lisa knew nothing about what had happened, but she simply couldn't shake from her mind the image of Guy flat on his back, pulling the cocky expression men get when they're being shagged. Keri knew she was acting suspiciously, but she simply couldn't relax. Having spent several days in denial, almost forgetting it had even happened, now, face to face with Lisa, Keri was struck by the horror of what she had done. She had actually slept with her best friend's boyfriend. She was the lowest of the low. She was scum.

She struggled to think what drove her to do it. Was it just that she had always desired Guy because he was one of the few men who she liked but who was unobtainable? Or had she done it out of frustration – as a subconscious act of revenge for Lisa's constant, intrusive meddling in her sex life? Had she allowed it to happen because the way she had seen Lisa treating

Guy reflected how Keri felt she, too, was treated? Perhaps she slept with Guy because she'd had enough of Lisa's stroppy self-obsession and was hoping to engineer a crisis in their friendship.

On the other hand, maybe she was just pissed.

Whatever it was that had been going through her head at the time, none of these reasons now made sense. Their argument at the party had already blown over. Keri didn't hate Lisa, and certainly didn't want their friendship to fall apart. But she had committed the worst possible betrayal. She had acted unforgivably. How she could possibly live with this – how she could ever feel comfortable in Lisa's company again – she didn't know.

Keri's tense behaviour had a curious effect on Lisa. It didn't instantly make her suspicious, but put her on the path which led in that direction. Lisa found herself looking at Keri and listening to her far more intently than usual. Her senses felt oddly alert. Between Keri and Josh and Guy, something strange had happened, and Lisa suddenly realized that it could, potentially, be unrelated to what she had done at the party.

She couldn't imagine the cause, but she felt she had sniffed out a hint of exclusion. Something had happened which Lisa didn't know about.

With this feeling creeping up on her throughout the meal, she only acknowledged it to herself at the moment when she began to home in on an answer.

As they started on dessert, it dawned on her that Keri hadn't asked after Guy. At a normal meal with Keri, this would be unusual. In the circumstances, it was bizarre. After their argument she had seemed more concerned about Guy than about her. Now, a week on, she hadn't mentioned him. She hadn't even shown any curiosity.

As this dim, unformed suspicion percolated into her brain, a casual question formed.

'Did you see Guy while I was away?'

Keri's chewing falters. She smiles at Lisa, and says, 'No. I phoned and he said you were away. We had a little chat. That's all.'

There was something in the pause before she spoke. Her smile, too, seemed a fraction false.

'Oh,' says Lisa, 'he said . . .' Lisa emphasizes the 'he', as if implying a contradiction. Again Keri flinches slightly, and her body seems to tense as she waits for the second half of the sentence. Registering this, Lisa finishes casually, '. . . you spoke.'

'Mmm,' says Keri. 'How is he?'

'Fine,' says Lisa. 'Fine.'

'He's not still . . . ?'

'What?'

'Upset about the party.'

'It was nothing. We were both just pissed. Everything's fine.'

'Good.'

'Isn't that what he said to you?' says Lisa.

'When?'

'On the phone.'

'Oh. Yeah. Pretty much. You know. He was upset, but . . . he knew it was nothing.'

'Well it was.'

'Good,' says Keri. She smiles, and swallows.

Lisa stares at her.

Wanting a little more time and space to think, Lisa turns away at the entrance to Piccadilly Circus Tube and hops over the road, past the stench of Burger King and round the corner into Shaftesbury Avenue, where she immediately spots a number 19 bus. It is some way down the street, opposite the Lyric Theatre, but the traffic is moving slower than walking pace and she barely needs to break stride to catch it.

Sitting at the front, on the top deck, observing the chaos of London from her serene vantage-point, Lisa's mind floats over and around the coming confrontation with Guy, her chest heavy with a knot of fear.

24

'Hi. No one's here, so leave a message. BEEP.'

'Hi . . . hi . . . hi. Keri. It's me. Graham. From the party. Guy and Lisa's party. Where we met. Outside the toilet. I . . . we . . . and the cab? I was in the cab with you. I'm . . . I'm . . . that's me anyway. And . . . bollocks . . . OK . . . I'll start again. The first thing to know is that I'm extremely cool and calm, and very articulate, and I don't have a stammer, *except* under unprovoked assault from an answerphone. In which case . . . on these rare occasions . . . you'll find that I do in fact talk shit. Unfortunately. OK. Right. But the point is, I'm Graham, and I'd like to take you up on your offer . . . or my offer, in fact . . . I'd like to take you up on my offer of agreeing to meet for a drink of coffee. Or tea. If that's what you prefer. But you're not in. As you're probably aware. So . . . if you like . . . you can phone me on . . . No. No. Forget it. It doesn't matter. I'll call again another time. But . . . er . . . OK. Bye.'

25

Although Lisa asks the question in a casual tone of voice, Guy senses immediately that it is loaded with significance. There is something artificial in her lightness of tone, and something strange in starting a conversation with such a direct question.

'Did you see Keri while I was away?' she says.

'Err . . . no.'

Guy flicks his eyes back to the TV, his mind racing. Lisa walks to the set, switches it off, and stands over him.

'No?' she says.

'No.'

'She says you did.'

'Oh. Right. Well – we bumped into each other. You know – briefly. We had a quick chat.'

'Face to face?'

'Yeah.'

'Not on the phone?'

'No.'

Lisa stares at him, not moving. The air in the room seems to thicken. Guy's heartbeat accelerates, and his body suddenly feels at once weightless and impossibly heavy. Still motionless, Lisa glares at him, her eyes moistening, then her face twitches and a tear rolls down her cheek.

She suddenly comes to life, wipes her face with a quick swipe of her sleeve, then steps towards Guy and grabs a fistful of hair. She yanks it backwards, pushing him on to his back, his head jammed into the corner of the sofa. Pinning him down by the hair, she holds her face up against his, and quietly asks, her features twisted with rage, 'What happened?'

Trembling with shock, Guy is unable to answer. He doesn't know what she knows. His mind feels utterly paralysed. He has never seen anyone look at him with such hatred.

'Let go,' he says, eventually.

She doesn't move. Her mouth tightens, as if she is about to spit in his face, and her grip on his hair strengthens.

'Get off!' he says, 'For fuck's sake!'

Still she doesn't move, so he puts his hand round her wrist and squeezes hard, his fingers digging in to the soft flesh around her tendons. She winces and relaxes her grip. He pushes her away, roughly, then stands, and the two of them square up to one another across the room.

'WHAT HAPPENED?' she yells.

'Can we just discuss this like –. . .'

'WHAT HAPPENED? DID YOU FUCK HER? DID YOU? DID YOU?'

Guy blinks, trying to summon a clear line of thought from his buzzing brain, but before he has spoken, he can see in Lisa's face that she has interpreted his silence as a yes.

'You did?' she says, softly.

Guy still can't answer. All strength seeps from his limbs as he sees Lisa rush across the room towards him. He watches a fist fly in his direction, as if in slow motion, then feels a painless jolt as it lands squarely in his eye socket. A sting of pain immediately follows, and he howls, clutching at his eye with an open palm. By the time he has uncovered his face, he is alone in the room.

He hears the slamming of cupboard doors and hobbles to the bedroom. Lisa is stuffing armfuls of clothes into a backpack.

'Lisa . . . look . . . please . . . it wasn't . . .'

She continues packing, seemingly unaware of his presence, then, head down, with a full bag on her back, she walks purposefully towards him. Guy is blocking her path in the doorway, but Lisa still doesn't look up. She pauses for a second, grabs his elbows, and knees him in the balls, feeling an odd spongy yielding before her kneecap crunches into his pelvis. Guy howls with pain.

With one hand over his left eye and the other cradling his scrotum, Guy slumps to the floor. All sensation vanishes behind an edifice of pain, until he hears the vicious crack of Lisa slamming her way out of the flat, followed by a cascade of footsteps and the muffled, resonant boom of the heavy outside door being venomously flung shut.

26

Lisa stamps into the street, her mind blank with rage. She storms purposefully to the Tube station, past the familiar rows of Victorian terraced houses, conscious that this route will no longer be one of the arteries of her life.

Outside the Tube station, she hesitates, suddenly realizing that she has no destination in mind. Then she is sitting on a bench by the bus stop, crying. *I've never cried in public before*, she thinks to herself. *I've never done this before.*

Passers-by stare at her – peering, she registers, with curiosity, not sympathy. No one stops, or says anything, or offers her a tissue.

Angry again, and pleased to be angry, she strides into the station, pulling her purse from her bag and her Tube pass from her purse. She flashes it at the ticket collector, and walks down to the trains – southbound platform. She can change at King's Cross and get the Northern line down to Clapham.

She doesn't quite know why, but she seems to be heading for Josh's flat.

Josh's first reaction, when he sees Lisa standing on his doorstep, is fear. She'd never normally turn up unannounced – no one ever just comes round without phoning first. Something must have happened. She must have found out what he's done.

They stare at one another in silence, neither even saying hello, before Lisa bursts into tears. Josh steps outside and puts an arm round her, still fearing that she has heard something from Helen. He pulls her into the flat, sits her on the sofa, gives her a box of tissues, and puts on the kettle.

When she stops crying and starts apologizing, he asks her what has happened.

'I've left Guy,' she says.

Josh almost crumples to the floor with relief. This isn't about him. He's still in the clear. His back turned, fiddling with tea-bags and mugs, he allows himself to close his eyes for a second and sighs, privately. Pouring the milk, he notices that his hands are trembling.

'Why?' he says, turning to look at Lisa. 'What happened?'

'He cheated on me.'

'What? Always?'

'No. Once. While I was away.'

'Oh. Right.'

An awareness that Josh, too, has slept with Keri stops Lisa volunteering the details. She doesn't mind telling him, but doesn't want to force it on him. She also doesn't want to think about it herself. Josh, it seems, doesn't feel he can ask.

'You just found out?' he says.

'Yeah.'

'And what happened?'

'I hit him and walked out.'

Put like this, it sounds ridiculous. Lisa exhales a sharp cackle, then dabs at her eyes with a tissue.

'For good?' says Josh, trying to conceal his surprise.

'Of course. I'm not going to put up with that.'

'No. No,' says Josh.

He doesn't understand. Sipping his tea, his hand still slightly trembly, the truth of what Lisa has told him sinks in for the first time. She has left Guy. She has done what he always prayed she would do. Although he finds it impossible to understand her motivation – it doesn't seem to make sense that such a long relationship could fall apart over something so minor – he doesn't want to probe. Lisa clearly isn't in any state for an interrogation. Besides, she had done the right thing to leave Guy. She was too good for him. Even if her reasons for ditching him were a little impulsive, she was making the right decision in the long run.

In all probability, though, the whole thing had been done in the heat of the moment and it wouldn't be long before Lisa changed her mind and went back home. Not wanting to engage in a conversation that could begin the process of Lisa talking herself out of what she had done, Josh decides to change the subject.

'I can put you up here,' he says. 'Until you get yourself sorted.'

'You don't mind?'

'I'll sleep on the sofa. You have my bed.'

'No. No way,' she says. 'I'll have the sofa. Honestly. I'd prefer it.'

'That's mad.'

'I'll be happier here. Really. I'm all restless.'

'You sure?'

'Positive.'

'OK. Just say if you change your mind.'

'Thanks. You're very kind.'

'You tired?' he says. 'You want to sleep now?'

'Err . . . I wouldn't mind. I can't really sustain a conversation.'

'I'll get you a sleeping bag.'

'This is really crap. Coming here like this. I'm sorry.'

'Don't be. I'm flattered.'

'Yeah, it's a real privilege to have a weeping, dribbling wreck turn up at your house and immediately pass out on the sofa.'

'It is,' he says. 'It is.'

She can see that he means it, and smiles. She has come to the right place. She was wrong to be angry with him. Josh is the only person who doesn't judge her. She feels safe in his house. She only has to tell him what she wants to tell. He won't ask too much, and at the end of it all, he will always think well of her. He is, without doubt, the kindest man she knows.

*

Lisa can't remember the last time she spent the night in a sleeping bag. She quickly feels sweaty, her skin prickling, itching against the bobbly fibres which have absorbed the night-sweats of Josh's other guests.

In the dark living room, one corner glowing green from the clock on the video, Lisa stares at the ceiling. Gaps are now beginning to open up in her anger, exposing a self-pity so deep it feels like a physical sensation. In the pit of her stomach, she feels a nausea of abandonment – a body-hollowing sadness – an invading vacuum of pure misery.

Never before, she realizes, has she actually been unhappy. She has never felt this. Guy and Keri have utterly humiliated her. She has been scorned and rejected by her two closest friends. Nothing she has ever done in her life has merited this treatment.

Lisa felt a naïvety fall away from her, liberating her from what seemed like one final vestige of childhood. Although things were bad with Guy for a long time, she had initially loved him without any reservations. This, she told herself, was something she never wanted to do again. It wasn't worth it. In an unjust world, you were a fool if you gave your life over entirely to another person, because whatever you did for them, you would never be able to predict what they might do to you. If you were dependent, you were one betrayal away from victimhood.

Lisa suddenly saw that she had always been attracted to people who were stronger than her. Keri and Guy were both more confident and self-assured than her, and Lisa had been drawn to them for this – in the hope that some of it would rub off on her. In the long run, it was now obvious, the opposite had happened. She had been their toy. They didn't respect her. They didn't need her. They judged her. They undermined her. And on a whim, they had humiliated and abandoned her.

A phase of her life had ended. She never wanted to see Keri or Guy again. She would start again, this time on her own terms.

27

'You fucking idiot,' says Graham, at the same time wondering why a grin is creeping across his face.

'I know. I know.'

'You fucking *idiot*!'

'I know.'

'You idiot!'

'I *know*! Will you stop saying that!'

'I just can't believe you're such an . . . an . . .'

'Idiot. Yeah. Thanks. I've got the point.'

'Five years, and you fuck it up for one shag.'

'It was kind of fucked up anyway. You might have noticed? Slight bit of tension at the party?'

'Couples do that all the time. Arguing's half the point.'

'Not in front of all your friends. Not as a speech. That's usually a bad sign.'

'You could have got over it, though.'

'Not now.'

'But you could have?'

'I don't reckon, to be honest.'

'So it was over anyway?'

'Probably.'

'And you got out of it quickly by shagging Keri.'

'Suppose so.'

'Maybe you're not such an idiot.'

'I am. Believe me. It was fucking stupid.'

'But you shagged Keri.'

'Yeah . . .'

'You *shagged* Keri.'

'True.'

'You're a genius. You pulled the old aggrieved-boyfriend, honorary-eunuch routine and just slipped it in when she was looking the other way. That's . . . that's . . .'

'Not what happened.'

'More or less, though. I mean, a woman like that would never shag you under normal circumstances.'

'What do you mean, normal circumstances?'

'You must have been . . . I don't know . . . about to cry or something clever like that.'

'I wasn't! I . . . I . . . actually I was. But it was genuine. It wasn't a trick. I wasn't trying to shag her.'

'That's what's so clever. Everyone wants to shag Keri. So the only way to turn her on is by acting like you don't want to shag her.'

'I didn't want to shag her.'

'Yeah, right.'

'I didn't. Not consciously. I mean, there's always a bit of residual ongoing desire, but that's normal. Everyone's got that. I didn't on that evening want to shag her any more than everyone does all the time anyway.'

'And then you did.'

'What?'

'Shag her.'

'Yeah.'

'You shagged her.'

'Yeah.'

'You fucking genius. You shagged Keri.'

'It wasn't genius. It just happened.'

'Just happened. I love that.'

'Graham –. . .'

'What was it like?'

'Please . . .'

'You have to tell me what it was like.'

'Just . . . you know.'

'I don't know. I really don't know. And I'm getting a boner just imagining what you're about to tell me.'

'Graham! Fuck off! It was all right. It was enjoyable. Not fantastic. But all right.'

'Not fantastic?'

'I mean, it *is* fantastic – it's not something you'd ever forget – but that's an ego thing. Not a physical pleasure thing.'

'She's no good? Is that what you're saying?'

'No! She's fine. It was nice. But a quim's a quim. And a new one never turns up quite where you expect. You get used to certain things. It's a bit of a fumble with someone new.'

'You fumbled? I can't believe you're telling me you fumbled! That's a crime. You're an idiot!'

'Will you make your mind up?'

'I . . . just . . . this whole thing is so weird. You've shagged Keri, and at the same time there's . . . I mean . . . you're single. All at once.'

'They are related.'

'It was a one-off with Keri, yeah?'

'Yes. Definitely.'

'So you're single. You're actually single.'

'Suppose I am.'

'You're never single.'

'I am now.'

'But that's not fair.'

'On who?'

'On you. It's ridiculous. You won't be able to cope. It's like letting a gerbil out of his cage. You're going to be all excited for about ten minutes, then you'll get all scared and want to be locked up again.'

'You've got a really healthy attitude to relationships.'

'I have. Avoid them. Look at you – you're a fucking wreck.'

'What do you expect? I've just spilt up with Lisa after five years! That's most of my adult life. I shared a flat with her. I did everything with her. If you weren't so obsessed with the whole Keri thing, you might have noticed that my whole life has basically come to an end!'

'Yeah. I was about to ask about that.'

'You just wanted to get the important stuff out of the way.'

'No – I was . . . you know . . . reacting to the shock elements first.'

'Well, thanks for your sympathy.'

'Look – Lisa wasn't that great, anyway.'

'What!?'

'She wasn't.'

'Graham! I was with her for five years! We split up yesterday! Can't you think of something more tactful to say?'

'What do you mean, more tactful? I've been holding it in for five years. If that isn't tact, I don't – . . .'

'It's just not what I need to hear. Save it for later.'

'It *is* what you need to hear. She wasn't so great. She was too stroppy. She hated my guts. You're better off without her.'

'I'm better off without her because she hated *your* guts.'

'Yeah. That's always a giveaway. Anyone who doesn't like me is obviously too uptight.'

'Lots of people don't like you.'

'Lots of people are too uptight. Lots of people shouldn't be your girlfriend.'

'But Lisa *was* my girlfriend. I liked her. And she didn't hate your guts. She just found you a bit boring.'

'That's worse. That means she's uptight *and* doesn't have a sense of humour.'

'Will you stop slagging off Lisa!'

'Why? She's chucked you! You're single. Fuck 'er.'

'How can you say that?'

193

'It's true. And it is what you need to hear. You're acting like you're all depressed because you think that's what you're supposed to do, but I can tell – you're not. You aren't. You're happy. The whole thing was going badly and you were dragging each other down and getting on each other's nerves and it was all difficult and painful, and now, suddenly, you're free. And into the bargain, you got to shag Keri. Of course you're happy. You *were* depressed. That was obvious. You've been a miserable git for months. And it was because of her. And now she's fucked off, and you're free. So you're not depressed any more.'

'You reckon?'

'Yeah. It's obvious.'

'Is it?'

'Not to you, it isn't. It's obvious to me, though.'

'You really think I'm not depressed?'

'I know you're not.'

'Actually . . . you . . . you might be right.'

'Course I'm right.'

'Now I think about it, I don't really . . . I mean . . . it doesn't actually feel *that* bad.'

'There you go, then. And she was uptight and she didn't have a sense of humour.'

'I suppose she was a bit prone to stress.'

'And to humourlessness.'

'She did have a sense of humour. It just didn't revolve around jokes.'

'What else is there?'

'Other stuff . . .'

'What? Custard pies? People falling over? Farts?'

'No . . .'

'There you go. Humourless.'

'Not exactly.'

'Forget her. Move on. You can do anything, now. You can shag anyone. Except Keri, obviously.'

'No. That wouldn't be very cool.'

'Course it would be cool. It would be great. She just wouldn't be up for it. She's out of your league. She took pity on you once. That was your lot.'

'You're jealous. It's so obvious you're jealous.'

'Course I am. You idiot. Course I'm jealous. You shagged Keri.'

'Will you stop saying that.'

'You shagged Keri.'

'Shut up.'

'You actually shagged her.'

'Shut up!'

'And you know what? If there's one word to describe how you feel about splitting up with Lisa, I bet I know what it is.'

'What? Guilty?'

'No.'

'Upset?'

'No.'

'Hurt?'

'No.'

'Remorseful?'

'No. Randy. You feel randy.'

'You reckon?'

'Maybe not quite yet, but soon. Take it from me.'

'As a man who never has a girlfriend and is always randy?'

'Exactly.'

'You're wrong. I feel kind of castrated at the moment. I'm not interested.'

'Castrated is Phase One. Phase Two is randy. It won't take long. Believe mc.'

28

At work, Lisa and Josh switched phones. Although this was extremely inconvenient, with every call being transferred between them, it was the only way Lisa felt able to relax. She had resolved to avoid all contact with Guy or Keri, and it was certain that sooner or later they would phone her. She didn't want to hear either of their voices, even just the word or two it would take for her to recognize them and hang up. More importantly, she didn't want them to hear her voice. She didn't even want them to hear her silence on the end of the phone, or measure the pace at which she hung up on them. They didn't deserve any access to her – they weren't to be allowed the satisfaction of being able to sense her anger or her misery.

The first time Guy phoned, Lisa felt a wave of tension sweep over the desk from Josh before he had even spoken. Then, as he calmly said, 'No, she doesn't want to speak to you,' Lisa's heart began to pump as if she was sprinting. Josh didn't look at her as he listened, then he said, 'No, I can't tell you that.'

Guy was probably asking where she was staying. She felt confident that even if he guessed that she was at Josh's flat (which was unlikely), Guy didn't know where that was. Keri also didn't know, and had almost certainly thrown away Josh's phone number, if she ever had it. Neither of them, she felt reasonably sure, even knew Josh's surname, so they wouldn't be able to look up his address.

As Josh's answers began to come in quicker succession – 'No', 'I'm afraid not', 'She's fine', 'No', 'No' – with an angry squeak beginning to be audible from his earpiece, the two of them began to look at each other, holding a direct stare, with a tiny smile forming in the corner of their mouths.

When Josh hung up, Lisa had to restrain herself from kissing him. He had pitched his answers with a calmness and courtesy perfect for maximizing Guy's frustration – hinting that he knew everything about Lisa's whereabouts and welfare, without ever giving away that she had told him to withhold the information.

Josh didn't need to tell her that Guy had worked himself up into a rage, and Lisa didn't need to thank him for this improvised cruelty. She was impressed with his skill, and delighted that he had so swiftly and unequivocally taken her side. One thing men like Josh certainly did learn at school was how to use politeness as a weapon.

By the end of the day, Guy and Keri had each phoned four times, in little flurries of activity which gave Lisa the impression that they were talking to each other between calling her. Josh quickly figured out that Keri was calling not just as a concerned friend, but as the joint culprit. This became so obvious that it was allowed to become clear that Josh understood without Lisa having to tell him, or him ever having to react. Between them, they chose to pretend that Josh didn't know who Keri was, other than an enemy of Lisa's.

Josh preserved his neutral tone with Keri, secretly relishing his position. Lisa had told him simply to inform her that she wanted Keri to leave her alone, and as he repeated this again and again down the phone to the increasingly distressed Keri, he felt that an injustice had been redressed. He had finally got under her skin. He had upset her. This was the perfect dignified, subtle revenge.

That night, lying awake, watching the green numbers on the video crawl their way through the night, Lisa, too, felt that she had somehow regained her dignity. Keri and Guy would have to live with their guilt until Lisa chose to absolve them. Which she would never do. In a sense, she was suddenly in control. There was a certain thrill in being wronged – an exhilarating righteousness which was pampered and fed by the guilt of Keri and Guy.

Although her body still felt wrung out with grief, there was now an odd sheen of power to her misery. There was nothing they could do to her that would make her feel worse. She, however, was in a position to tug and nag at their guilt, goading them to swallow an ever greater share of her unhappiness.

29

'Er . . . hi . . . er . . . you're not in . . . again . . . but
. . . er . . . it's Graham again . . . and . . . er . . . I was
just wondering if you'd like to go to the cinema some
time to see . . . er . . . a film. Er . . . O K . . . bye.'

'Hi . . . my number's 0171–206–1846. I forgot to say.
Sorry. O K. Er . . . bye.'

'That was me again, by the way. Graham. I forgot to
say. The number – it wasn't just a random person
without a name phoning up to give their number. It
was me. Er . . . O K. Bye. If I've forgotten anything
else I'll call again in a couple of minutes.'

30

Graham was wrong. Randy never happened. Depressed did.

Alone in the flat, Guy's initial failure to marshal any genuine misery over the sudden disappearance of Lisa slipped away. He began to veer between moping, lovelorn aches of loneliness, and a sneaking acid hatred for Lisa that could somehow coexist with an inability to fall out of love with her. He resented the fact that in a subtle way – a way he would never be able to get anyone to understand – she had tricked him.

In the wake of their break-up, he saw the preceding months with a new clarity. Lisa, he was now certain, had spent this time slowly and deliberately undermining their relationship, preparing it for a collapse, waiting for Guy to carelessly do something that would cause it to crumble in his hands. Lisa wanted to leave him, and had been edging herself away from Guy for a long time. It was as if she'd been standing on the threshold with her bags packed for months, delaying her exit until she had the moral high ground.

It was Lisa who had destroyed their relationship, not him. She had wired it up and planted the explosives, then waited round the corner until Guy tripped over the detonator.

He knew that sleeping with Keri had been an awful mistake. He knew there was no excuse for his unfaithfulness. He simply resented the fact that because of this single slip-up, all the blame for their separation was being placed at his feet. Lisa had got exactly what she wanted – she had left Guy – and she had pulled it off with a piece of typically convenient double-think which allowed her to feel wronged and helpless. As usual, Lisa had got her own way, with her delusions of weakness intact.

Lisa loved feeling wronged. Aside from anything else, it allowed her to get angry – and anger was Lisa's hobby. She had mastered the phrasing, instrumentation, dynamic control, pacing, breathing technique and tonal colouring required to generate symphonic masterpieces of rage.

The most impressive aspect of her genius for anger was that she could somehow use it in a manner that allowed no comeback. She could always pitch it at a level which inhibited a response – sometimes coming on so strong that she flattened Guy into submission, at other times using silence and tears like a scalpel, dissecting opposition into benign sympathy. Somehow, if Guy ever managed to get a grievance off his chest, it would always be swamped, swept aside, exploded or simply forgotten under assault from Lisa's emotional arsenal. This time, she was using a full retreat to hammer home her victory. She had won the battle, secured a favourable settlement and retired to a hidden bunker before Guy had even recovered from being kicked in the balls.

What galled him more than anything was that he couldn't say any of this. She wasn't giving him the opportunity to tell her that he saw through her self-deception. It seemed like one last insult, after all she had done to him, that she was allowing herself to think she was blameless. Most infuriating of all was that she had recruited her moron of a colleague as the smuggest and most obtuse of personal bodyguards.

Guy did feel guilty, and regretted sleeping with Keri (or tried to), but as time passed, he found his guilt sheathed by a protective layer of resentment. In this, their final confrontation, he was determined not to be outmanoeuvred by Lisa. When she came out of hiding – when she eventually realized she had to talk to him to negotiate a way of dividing their possessions – he would make sure he got through to her that she hadn't won. They had betrayed one another equally. They were both in the wrong.

He knew all her tricks, and if there was one thing he could guarantee, it was that he would find a way of matching her anger. He wouldn't placate her, and he wouldn't be steam-rollered. He would say his piece.

Stepping in after an unproductive day in the library, Guy instantly sensed that something had happened to the flat. A whiff of emotional napalm hit his nostrils in the hallway. Lisa had visited.

The living room was half empty. Literally. Lisa had taken half of everything. One lamp, two chairs, a rug, the TV, the phone and a table had gone – leaving one lamp, no chairs, a sofa, no rug, the stereo, the answerphone and a coffee-table behind. Precisely half the books (the top two shelves) and half the CDs (the bottom shelf-and-a-half) had also gone. Owing to Guy's rather anal shelving technique, this meant that he had lost all his books from A to L, and all his CDs from M to Z.

In the kitchen, half the crockery, half the cutlery and half the pans had gone. In the bedroom, Lisa had seemingly compensated for the bulkiness of the wardrobe and bed by taking everything else – even the duvet and bedlinen. The previously crammed bathroom was stripped bare, its single long shelf exposed to daylight for the first time in years, now carrying three stranded-looking items – a toothbrush, a razor and a can of shaving foam. It was this room that somehow seemed the most decimated, though it occurred to Guy that this was perhaps the only place where Lisa had taken nothing that didn't belong to her.

Back in the living room, Guy noticed a note on the floor where the table used to be, held down by a set of keys to the flat. He picked it up and read:

Don't try and find where I'm living. Don't phone me at work. Don't ever attempt to contact me. You betrayed me. You disgust me. Fuck you.

Lisa, it appeared, had won.

31

Graham was pursuing Keri more out of instinct than from any genuine belief that he might actually get her – rather in the way dogs chase rabbits. However, since hearing that Guy had succeeded in shagging her (albeit through devious means), it had occurred to Graham for the first time that she might, just might, in the long run, be obtainable.

Although she was perfect in areas of the body that Graham had never even noticed were capable of perfection – her ears, for instance, were distinctly sexy – and was also perfect in terms of how they got on (that is, she found him funny), it had still not dawned on Graham that seduction might be a possibility until he heard about Guy's achievement.

Keri was, simply, a different species. She belonged to the Beautiful People – the élite group who are allowed on posters, magazine covers and cinema screens. Guy and Graham belonged to the Ordinary People – who look bad enough in the flesh, and even worse through any kind of lens. Graham knew that BPs sometimes liked to have the odd OP as a friend, but cross-breeding always seemed out of the question.

Your friendship could always be seen as long-term groundwork for mental crack-ups, industrial accidents or other kinds of disfigurement that might, in a weak moment, cause them to forget which species they belonged to, but this hope had to be kept at bay. Just having a BP as a friend was a privilege, with an unspoken sense of possibility floating in the background as an endless source of secret excitement.

Guy, however, was more ordinary than Graham. His nose was too big for a start. And if she'd made the mistake once, she might slip up again. Unless, of course, she'd learnt her lesson. Guy was hardly the ideal ambassador for the OPs. He took himself far too seriously, and wasn't nearly relaxed enough to be much of a lay. Moreover, on his own admission, in this, his personal Superbowl Final of sexual congress, he'd fumbled. And if that was *his* version of events, then the sheer depth of his sexual failure was almost beyond imagining.

In fact, the more he thought about it, the more Graham convinced himself that although Keri's encounter with Guy made her seem more obtainable, it had in fact put her further out of reach than ever. Guy had ruined everything. As a known friend and ally of the culprit, Graham was a fumbler by association. The industrial accident/mental collapse route represented his only chance of getting her. He was going to have to play the long game.

Still, he had discreetly upped the stakes from a coffee to the cinema, and she had accepted. Nominally, though, it wasn't a date. He hadn't phrased it as a date. They were just two people who had met at Guy's party, who happened to get on, who coincidentally belonged to opposing genders.

For this reason, Graham suggested a late-ish (i.e., post-food) showing of a film which would leave them just enough time for a couple of drinks in the pub. He wasn't going to risk one of those three-hour first-date conversations which are the social equivalent of a November cross-country run. No – this wasn't a date. There was no way she'd fancy him. They were just going to be mates. A film, a quick chat in the pub, then straight home for a wank.

'So,' says Keri, sinking an inch of her pint, 'how is he?'

'Who?' says Graham.

'Guy.'

'Oh, Guy. Yeah. He's fine.'

'Is he?'

'Yeah.'

'What – the whole Lisa thing hasn't –. . . ?'

'Oh, the *Lisa* thing. Right. Sorry. Yeah. He's miserable.'

'Is he?'

'Yeah.'

'Really?'

'Well – he's trying to be.'

'*Trying* to be miserable?'

'Yeah. Last time we spoke, anyway.'

'Why's he trying to be miserable?'

'Oh, you know what Guy's like. He thinks too much. He convinced himself that what he did was unforgivable and set about making himself feel crap, even though he's actually well shot of Lisa and is probably relieved to be on his own.'

'He's relieved to be on his own?'

'No. He's miserable. But he ought to be relieved to be on his own. And he would be if he didn't waste all his time feeling guilty.'

'You think he's better off without her?'

'Probably. Yeah.'

'You didn't like her?'

'Err . . . you know. We never saw eye to eye.'

Keri shrugs and smiles to herself – an odd, sad little smile of recognition.

'Maybe you saw a different side of her,' says Graham.

'Maybe.'

Graham takes a large slug of beer, anxious to think of a way to draw the conversation away from the awkward subject of his dislike for Lisa. He can't tell whether anything is left of Keri's friendship with her, and doesn't want to say the wrong thing. 'You're not talking to Guy, then?' he says. 'I mean, since you're asking me how he is.'

'We spoke a bit at first, when we were trying to get through to Lisa, but not now. Feels too weird.'

'What – is there still . . . ?'

'No. There's nothing. It just doesn't feel right to talk to him.'

'Why?'

''Cause Lisa's not talking to either of us.'

'So?'

'It just doesn't feel right.'

''Cause you make each other feel more guilty?'

'Yeah. Suppose so.'

'You feel guilty?'

'Course I do.'

'Badly?'

'Terribly. You forgotten what I did?'

'No, but . . . guilt doesn't exactly get you very far, does it?'

'It's better than not feeling guilty. If I couldn't even accept that what I did was wrong, and deal with that, then I wouldn't be much of a human being, would I?'

'I think you'd be a lot of a human being, whatever you did.'

'I'm not joking,' she says, trying not to smile. She doesn't want to be seen falling for such crude flirtation. 'I did an awful thing.'

'Maybe it's not so awful,' he says. 'You helped them get away from each other, which is what they both needed.'

'That doesn't make my part in it any less bad.'

'Why not? Everyone's better off now than they were then.'

'It was wrong. There's no excuse.'

'I'm sure we can find one if we look hard enough.'

'That's stupid. I don't want one. I've just got to . . . you know . . . get used to the fact that I'm not such a great person.'

'Don't say that.'

'Why not?'

'You are a great person.'

'You don't know me.'

'I can tell. It's obvious.'

'Graham – thanks, but amateur flattery isn't going to help me get over what I did.'

'What are you talking about? That was professional flattery. Amateur flattery's when I tell you you're in the right because you've got nice tits.'

'I thought that's what you did just say.'

Graham laughs, surprised to be bested. 'OK. Maybe it was a bit amateur.'

'Look – whatever you think of my tits, I did an awful thing. If I didn't suffer for it afterwards, that would make me an even worse person than I am anyway.'

'Why d'you do it, then? If it was so awful? If you're going to let it ruin your life?'

'Don't know. It was stupid. I just . . .'

'Just what?'

'Don't know. I was just there, and Guy was so upset, and I just . . . you know . . .'

'Felt sorry for him.'

'Yeah.'

'Hah!'

'What?'

'Nothing. Sorry.'

'I mean, it wasn't pity, or anything.'

'No?'

'I just . . . you know . . . I thought Lisa had been treating him like shit, and I knew she was in the process of dumping him, but he wasn't facing up to it, and we both got drunk, and I've always liked him anyway, and in my head I already knew I'd . . . sort of . . . changed sides . . . and that felt like such a bad thing to do to Lisa that . . . that whether I took it further or not didn't seem to make too much difference. I was drunk. It was so stupid.'

'And you felt sorry for him?'

'You know – sympathy. If someone you like is suddenly unhappy, and they let you in on that, it brings you a lot closer.'

'Of course,' says Graham, filing that information away for future reference. Guy may look like a loser, he thinks, but he's a cunning, sneaky little bastard when there's a shag in the offing. 'And . . . er . . . now you're not talking?'

'She won't take my calls and I don't know where she's living.'

'To Guy, I mean.'

'No. There's nothing to say. We've both just got to sort things out with Lisa. If we communicate behind her back, it feels like we're making the whole thing worse.'

'And how are you going to sort things out with Lisa?'

'Don't know.'

'She going to forgive you?'

'Doubt it.'

'So what are you waiting for?'

'Don't know,' says Keri, her head drooping, her eyes moistening slightly. 'Don't know.'

Graham, intimidated by this show of emotion, shuffles his feet and offers Keri another drink.

Holding a tenner in the air he slumps against the bar, his legs suddenly unable to support him under the sheer weight of lust coursing heavily through his body. During their conversation it has occurred to Graham for the first time that on top of all her other attributes, Keri actually has human emotions – including the horniest possible smattering of Juliette Binoche-style melancholia – that even-an-earth-shaking-orgasm-wouldn't-cheer-me-up look in the eyes that makes you just want to tear a woman's clothes off and prove her wrong.

She's perfect. She's beyond perfect. She's so far out of reach he should be put on medication for even thinking about shagging her.

32

A week is more than enough to spend in a sleeping bag. On the seventh night at Josh's house, with the video telling her it is two in the morning, Lisa kicks aside her restrictive, uncomfortable cocoon, slips off the sofa and walks upstairs.

She opens the door to Josh's bedroom and watches the rise and fall of his chest as he sleeps, listening to his ponderous other-worldly breathing. He is curled up, his face hidden from view, on the far side of his double bed. Without questioning what she is doing, or pausing to consider the consequences of her action, Lisa quietly slides in beside him, nuzzling against his back for warmth.

The scale and solidity of a man's body under her fingers instantly makes her feel better. Ever since taking her share of possessions from the flat, she had felt strangely weak. She regretted succumbing to such an obvious act of revenge, and sensed that this had somehow lost her the upper hand. Against all her instincts, she had shown Guy her anger, and had therefore weakened her position. Feeling more miserable and lonely than ever, a broad male back in a warm, wide bed was exactly the comfort she needed.

Josh wriggles in her arms, lets out a half-waking

sniff, then she feels his body jerk and immediately stiffen in her arms.

He is suddenly wide awake. His eyes, hidden from Lisa's view, flash open as soon as he realizes what has happened. Although he tries not to give any reaction, he can't stop his body cramping with fear.

Since the incident with Helen, Josh hasn't thought about women or sex. He hasn't even masturbated. He has simply existed: working, sleeping, and using television as a psychological anaesthetic. Now, suddenly, the woman he loves is in his bed.

His mind pulsing with anxiety and confusion, battling to hold at bay memories of what he did to Helen, revolted by the seedy tingle of his erection, the night passes more slowly than any other night of his life. Awake, on his side, facing away from Lisa, he simply stares at the window, praying for a glimmer of dawn.

*   *   *

Lisa's possessions were piled in the corner of Josh's living room, waiting for her to find a new flat. Over the next few weeks, the tower of boxes began to shrink as various implements, clothes, CDs, toiletries and gadgets came into use around Josh's flat. Somehow it became apparent that Lisa wasn't leaving.

More than anything, Lisa loved Josh's physical timidity. This well-built, strong man was utterly at her command. Sexually and socially, he never demanded anything of her. He seemed almost in awe of her, loving everything she did to him and for him, never pressing her to do anything she didn't explicitly request. For nights on end, they slept in the same bed, with Josh not once attempting to take advantage of her unhappiness or vulnerability.

Only ever so slowly, and at a speed dictated by Lisa, did sex begin to creep in. She gradually went beyond simply holding him, and began to caress him, patiently and gently, long into the night. Although she could feel him trembling with arousal, and could sense a bulging, twitching erection, he never once tried to accelerate the pace. He barely even touched her with his hands.

Lisa took this as a clever sex-game. Josh knew she had been hurt, and he was allowing her to dictate the rules, slowly drawing her back towards sexual self-confidence by silently, passively assuring her that she was in control.

For this insight she loved and admired him.

And the more he played the game, the more she desired his body.

When, at last, she allowed herself to hold and rub his penis, she instantly felt a spark of lust in her crotch. Feeling his erection in her hand: large, rigid and hot, she rolled him on to his back and straddled him. Within seconds, he came inside her.

The following day, she bought a pack of condoms.

33

Awake in the middle of the night, staring round his bare bedroom, a new resentment popped into Guy's head. He hadn't heard from Helen. Not since the anniversary party – and barely even then – had Guy spoken to her.

It seemed impossible that in the intervening time Helen could have failed to hear what had happened. And even if, through some feat of seclusion, she had missed the news of Guy's separation from Lisa, the events of that evening alone should have been enough to prompt a phonecall.

But no, Helen was in one of her silent phases – which inevitably meant that she was having a good time and didn't need Guy to cheer her up or jolly her along. For years, Guy had protected and looked after Helen, piecing her together after trauma upon trauma. Now, finally, Guy had problems of his own, and Helen had vanished.

His loneliness, he realized, stemmed not only from the loss of Lisa, but also from a feeling that his break-up had left him almost friendless. He wasn't a needy person. For years, he hadn't demanded anything of his friends. Now, for once, they had a chance to do something for him, and he had barely received a single phonecall. For the first time he could remember in his adult life he needed sympathy and comfort, but there was none to be had. His friends had disappeared. No one had come forward to give Guy what he wanted and, he felt sure, deserved.

His friendships suddenly seemed thinner and more selfish than ever before. He had allowed a narrow collection of people to become a substitute for family simply because they were good company, and now, in a phase of depression and weakness, it seemed like a poor trade-off. Everyone was too busy; London was too big and crowded; no one could be expected to *notice* anything about your life. You had to go out and get sympathy – you had to feel strong enough to tell people what was wrong and to demand comfort. If you really felt low this was the last thing you could countenance doing, so you would be left on your own to stew.

Friendship on demand felt like no friendship at all. A collection of peers speckled around a large city simply didn't amount to any kind of safety net. No one cared. And only when you were miserable did you acquire the clarity of insight to see just how alone you were.

On a masochistic level, Guy almost felt pleased to be so unhappy. Only now, through a lens of depression, was he seeing what his life really amounted to. Keri was avoiding him; Graham was congenitally incapable of providing any kind of genuine sympathy; Lisa had vanished from his life; and Helen, his closest friend, had chosen to let him down. There was no one else with whom Guy wouldn't worry that his unhappiness simply made him boring company. For all the swirling, messy rampage of thoughts which perpetually fizzed around his head, Guy felt he had nothing to say for himself. If he went out and tried to socialize in an ordinary way with ordinary people, he knew he would embarrass himself. There was only one thing he genuinely wanted to talk about, and it certainly didn't constitute social chit-chat. Aside from that, his mind was a blank. Everything else had been swept aside by his gloom. And the minute you were a burden – the minute you were in need – you were on your own. If you couldn't entertain anyone, no one wanted to see you.

Only one corner of Guy's brain resisted this fog of despair. A glimmer in the back of his mind pulsed feebly with the notion that there might be a reason for Helen's absence. If she was on a down rather than an up – if something had happened to her – then it was possible that she had been sitting at home engulfed by precisely the same feelings of abandonment as Guy.

His hurt at being let down by his friends centred, he realized, on Helen. He didn't actually expect anyone else to care deeply about what happened to him. Other than Lisa, Helen was the only person with whom he shared any genuine intimacy. No one else had actually failed him, since he didn't really have any expectations of his other friends. His feelings of abandonment came down to the fact that he had always thought there were two women who loved him, and now they had both left him at the same time.

If something had happened to Helen, maybe his despair stood a chance of seeming groundless. It would have to be something bad, however. A summer cold wouldn't exactly be enough to explain away her lack of concern for his welfare.

Nervously, Guy picked up the phone and dialled Helen's number, hoping and not hoping that something awful had befallen her.

34

For their fifth date, Graham took Keri bowling. The instant she stepped into Rowan's Superbowl in Finsbury Park, she knew this was not an experience she would ever repeat. Apart from anything else, everyone in the building was wearing blue shoes. And within minutes, an overweight man with oil-slick hair was insisting that Keri, too, hand over her trainers and join the blue-shoe club.

When Keri refused, Graham stared at her as if she was mad.

'What do you mean, "no"?' he says, passing his shoes over the counter.

'Which part of the word don't you understand?'

'But you can't bowl without bowling shoes.'

'Why not?'

'You just can't.'

'Why?'

'It's the rules. They don't let you.'

'Have you asked why?'

'You . . . you don't have to. It's how it works. No one bowls without the shoes.'

'But they're blue,' she says. 'And they've got leather soles. Shoes like this ought to be illegal.'

'It's part of the sport. If you feel like an idiot before

you've even picked up a bowling ball, then there's only so much worse things can get when you start trying to throw it.'

'That doesn't make any sense.'

'Of course it doesn't make sense. Now give me your shoes.'

The ball weighed about as much as a suitcase for a two-week holiday. Having just about achieved a backswing, Keri let the weight of the ball swing her arm forwards. Her thumb sticking in one of the holes, the ball gave her shoulder an aggressive yank before flying up above her head, then landing with a resonant boom that caused everyone in the adjacent ten lanes to stare in her direction. The ball at first didn't seem to move at all, then, slowly, it began to roll downhill towards the pins.

The whole concept of sport was lost on Keri. On the rare occasions she came across football on TV, it always looked to her like tropical fish in a tank. First they all went up one end, then they all went down the other end, and there seemed to be no logic governing these movements. It didn't seem possible to predict which direction they would all run in next, yet whole roomfuls of viewers jumped around, groaned and howled as if their lives were at stake.

Likewise, even though she understood the principle of bowling – it didn't take great intelligence to grasp the idea that knocking down a large number of skittles was better than knocking down a small number of skittles – when it came to precisely why you should care how many distant lumps of wood you had toppled over, Keri was utterly lost. And as for the urge to knock down more skittles than the person you had come with, that would have to be filed with all other sporting competitiveness as one of the great mysteries of human nature. If you could give anything at all a number, it seemed, people would start calling it a score, and would start trying to get a bigger number than their friends. It was all extremely strange.

This thought process was interrupted by Graham suddenly grabbing her round the waist, lifting her off her feet, and yelping in her ear. Her instant reaction, overriding even her bewilderment, was a rush of pleasure. Maintaining her balance by gripping his arms, she could feel his muscles tense with the effort of holding her weight, revealing a few bulges she had never known were there. He could lift her as easily as she could lift a cat. Underneath those geeky clothes was a decent body. He was doing his best to hide it, but the man had distinct physical potential.

'What are you doing?' she says, when he puts her down. Although Keri never blushes – blushing isn't something she approves of – she is annoyed to feel a patch of heat rise from her neck to her cheeks.

'Nine! Nine!'

Following Graham's finger, extended down the lane in front of her, Keri sees one skittle standing alone next to the gutter, in the same spot where there had been a large clump of them a few moments ago.

'And you've still got another throw!' he continues, excitedly. 'If you get that one it's a spare.'

'Oh,' says Keri.

He has already explained twice what a spare is, and what effect it has on your score, but Keri has already forgotten. From his tone of voice, she can tell it must be something good. She is clearly supposed to want a spare.

Her next ball rattles noisily down the gutter on the opposite side of the lane to the skittle she is supposed to be aiming at.

Graham smiles at her when she turns back to him. 'It's still nine,' he says, encouragingly. 'That's good.'

She shrugs and nods, trying to give the impression that she gives a toss.

The only disappointment in his reaction to her successful throw was that he had been watching her skittles at all. Hitherto, she had assumed he was treating the game in the same way as her – as a sport designed specifically to provide lengthy scrutiny of your prospective sexual partner's arse. The scoring system was clearly just an embellishment for the sake of decency. Tenpin bowling, it seemed obvious, was just the cover for a game called Check Out My Wares. And for Graham to have even noticed that she'd knocked down nine skittles meant he wasn't playing properly.

On the performance side of Check Out My Wares, however, he was giving it his all. He bowled with a neat little wiggle, and the wares on display were significantly better than Keri had given him credit for. The trousers would have to go, but the arse – the arse was great.

Previously, by the time she ever got round to lusting after anyone, she had already slept with them. Now, for the first time ever, Keri was fantasizing about a man who had so far given no indication of even noticing that she was female.

He took her to play kinky sex games in blue leather shoes, they talked on the phone almost every day, half their time together seemed to be spent laughing, and yet Graham gave no indication of wanting to get her into bed. He barely touched her, and when they parted, he did so with a dry peck on the cheek. In fact, now she thought about it, Graham was giving off clear and unambiguous signals. He wasn't interested. He was single and male, but not interested. His manner was asexual. He liked her and enjoyed her company, but didn't want to sleep with her.

Which was fine. If that's the way he had been plumbed in, there was nothing Keri could do about it. Other than entering a convent and weeping for six months.

After several years of turning men down, she had finally met someone she liked, and for no apparent reason, he wasn't interested. He wanted to be her friend. He was more interested in her bowling ability than in her arse. He was a eunuch.

It wasn't fair. It simply wasn't fair.

35

The moment Helen's flatmate, Nicola, answered the phone, Guy knew Helen was in trouble. After a brief outburst of undirected anger, Nicola explained that Helen had disappeared from the flat without even leaving a note and without paying her rent. She had taken a few clothes with her, but the majority of her possessions had been left behind while Nicola went further and further into debt, until she persuaded Helen's parents to clear the room. Nicola was too angry about the money she had lost to give any clear sense of exactly when this had happened, and refused to acknowledge that Helen's behaviour was at all worrying or even to debate what might have prompted her to run away.

Guy put the phone down, his heart pumping, adrenalin suddenly blurring his mind. The news that Helen had vanished, strangely, felt like more of a confirmation than a revelation, and Guy was both relieved and horrified. Helen's life always teetered on the brink of disaster, and Guy had an awful feeling that the worst had now happened.

After retrieving an old address book, Guy phones Helen's family home. It is her mother who answers.

'Hi. Er . . . I'm Guy, a friend of Hel–. . .'

'Do you know where she is?' the mother snaps, cutting Guy off.

'No. No. That's what I was phoning to ask you.'

'You haven't heard any news?' she insists.

'No.'

'You don't know anyone else who knows anything?'

'No.'

'Do you have phone numbers of people who might know something?'

'Er . . . possibly.'

'Who? Give me their names. When did you last see her?'

'A few weeks ago. She . . . can you tell me what's happened? I'm a close friend of hers. I was just worried because I haven't heard from her.'

'She what? You said "she".'

'Nothing. I was just going to say she was at a party. I haven't seen her since then.'

'What party? Who was she with? Did you see who she left with?'

'Has something happened? Is she OK?'

'Who did she leave with?'

'I don't know. I barely saw her. I know she was there, but there was a lot of stuff going on. I didn't see who she was with.'

'Whose party was it?'

'Mine.'

'Do you have a list of who was invited?'

'Not a list. I know who was there.'

'Please. Give me their names and numbers.'

'All right. But will you tell me what's happened? Do you . . . do you think she's OK?'

A long, breathy silence comes down the phone line.

'Is . . . do you not know anything?' continues Guy. 'Has she disappeared? Is this . . . are the police . . . ?'

'Not interested. They're not interested. The minute they discovered she packed a bag before she left, they ditched the whole thing. They don't count you as disappeared unless you've been abducted. And for some reason they think you can't be abducted if you happen to be carrying a suitcase. They said if they followed up everyone who took an unplanned holiday, they'd never have time to do anything else.'

'But you think something's happened?'

'Yes. Yes. We know it has. She wouldn't do this. She wouldn't do this.'

'You don't know anyone who's seen her?'

'Nicola gave us a few names, but they didn't really mix with the same people. She took her address book with her. We looked through all her things, and . . . there was no record of anything. There was no sign of . . . of . . . She lived in one room with a few clothes and books and CDs and that's all there was. We don't know what she does – who she spends time with. We know the first names of a few of her friends, but that's all. We . . . that's almost the worst thing. We've got all her things in our house now, and it doesn't tell us anything about her, except that we didn't know who she was. Who she is. We don't know anything about her. We never even noticed how secretive she was. We . . . we . . .'

Guy hears the clunk of the receiver being put on a table, and a few muffled sobs. He listens, suddenly noticing that his hands are white and cold. A rustling noise and the faint sound of breath lets him know that Helen's mother is back on the line, not speaking.

Guy breathes back at her, trying to think of something to say.

'I can tell you,' he says, his voice catching in his throat. 'I knew . . . I know her well. We . . . see each other once or twice a week. I can give you the names and numbers of everyone at the party. I can help. Honestly. I'll phone everyone for you, and find out if there's any news. Someone might have heard something. But I haven't seen her since she . . . went away. And I don't know anyone who has. If she hasn't contacted you, and she hasn't contacted me, I don't think we can hold out much hope that she will have phoned anyone else. But I'm sure she's fine. I'm sure she's fine.'

Again, Helen's mother is crying on the other end of the phone line, this time still listening to Guy – her splutters and chokes now loud in his ear.

'She's much stronger than she seems,' he says. 'I'm sure she's fine. She'll be fine. I'm sure.'

36

'Go on top of me.'

'What?'

'I want you on top of me.'

Without releasing him from the grip of her thighs, Lisa rolls on to her side, then her back, one hand pressed against Josh's arse, preventing him from slipping out of her.

She kisses him deeply on the lips, then lies back and closes her eyes, shifting her legs to pull him deeper inside her. She feels his motionless cock, slightly shrunk from their manoeuvre, begin to grow again in her depths.

Josh stares at Lisa, frozen. Although they have now had sex many times, she has never yet made him go on top. She has never, in fact, made him do anything. Which was the whole point. If you don't have to do anything, you can't do anything wrong.

Now, looking down at her, Josh feels paralysed by fear and memory. A moment of pleasure at feeling her deep wetness is pushed aside by a rising nausea of guilt. Feeling his erection dwindle, he instinctively begins to rock his body against hers – gently at first – just enough to keep himself hard. With Lisa underneath him, demanding action, and a condom in place which will slip off if he allows his concentration to waver, Josh closes his eyes, focuses his attention, and begins to thrust with a regular, sustainable, slow beat around which he attempts to hypnotize his thoughts.

As Lisa begins to moan with pleasure, the buzz in Josh's brain dwindles and fades. And as his mind clears, his rhythm accelerates, willing them towards orgasm – one of which suddenly arrives with a shudder and quick squirt of bliss, grabbing Josh by the back of the neck and squelching his brain in a moment of pure, unselfconscious release.

Then, suddenly, he is crying. His penis shrinking with each heartbeat, still inside her, Josh's body begins to shake and tremble as tears roll down the side of his nose and tickle his lips.

Pinching the condom between finger and thumb, he pulls out, drops the soggy rubber membrane on to the floor, and rolls aside, curling himself up – facing away from Lisa – ashamed and confused by this humiliating rush of unmediated emotion.

'What?' says Lisa, wrapping her body around him. 'What is it? What's wrong?'

For weeks, ever since the evening with Helen, Josh had felt that his life was in some way over. He had feared that he would have to be celibate for years to come. In his core, he had lost all interest in sex. Only by avoiding women completely would he be able to keep his self-hatred at bay. Now, against his wishes,

Lisa had infiltrated herself into his life, and had somehow dragged him back.

Wiping his eyes, cradled by Lisa, her fingers combing and twining through his chest hairs, he realizes, with a stab of surprise, that his tears aren't the product of this self-loathing, or even of his guilt. They are, quite simply, tears of relief.

He rolls over to face her, suddenly no longer ashamed. 'I love you,' he says. 'I absolutely love you.'

'Good,' she replies, stroking his forehead.

'I need you. I always want to be with you.'

'Good,' she says again. 'I'm pleased.'

Looking at her beautiful face, feeling her fingers sweep through his hair, Josh feels a renewed surge of certainty. Lisa is everything he needs. His struggle is over. Her typhoons of emotion – her demands and her noise – are precisely what make her so perfect. All Josh has to do is keep up, and remain sympathetic. He doesn't have to work her out or impose himself on her. He must simply do what is asked of him.

While she has been in his flat, he has been happier and more self-assured than at any time in his life. With Lisa, and only with Lisa, the pressure is off. He doesn't have to continue attempting to define himself. She creates such a powerful universe that he can exist in her gravity – as a planet to her sun.

He now sees that this is the only way he can ever be happy – living to the rhythm of someone else.

His need for her, he realizes, is absolute. She represents his last and only chance. He can't trust himself to live the rest of his life without an external force to frame and moderate his actions. He can't, in fact, trust himself enough to allow her ever to leave him on his own again. Only with Lisa is he safe from the side of him that assaulted Helen. He doesn't want to face any more self-examination, and with Lisa in his life, he won't have to. Her needs, her desires, her demands, her noise can form a focus for his future.

'Marry me,' he says.

'What?'

'Marry me. Please. I want to marry you.'

'Why?'

'We make each other happy. We can be happy together. What we've got is perfect. It couldn't be any better. We care for each other – we look after each other – we should be together. For good. I'll never leave you or betray you. Please.'

Lisa looks at him, his face still puffy and moist with tears, and smiles. An initial horror at the thought of being married to Josh – at the thought of making any kind of commitment which resembles the one she has just escaped – rapidly fades into a confusion of conflicting desires.

Lisa felt, more than anything else, deeply unhappy. Her initial anger at Guy had been unable to sustain itself over recent weeks, weakening into a cold, biting hatred for him which had none of the cathartic powers of her fading rage. Simply hating Guy did nothing to make her feel any better.

Her poisonous thoughts now simply stewed inside her, without release, contaminating her moods and sapping her energy. Never before had she been so low, or even understood that misery was, in fact, crushingly boring.

With the weeks bleeding together, the process of grieving over her lost relationship was beginning to seem endless. She was tired of unhappiness, and of an existence which seemed so static. There was no apparent escape route. Only through a radical life-change would she be able to get away from her pain, yet nothing had occurred to her. In a lethargy of depression, she knew she had to *do* something to shake herself out of it, but she simply didn't have the physical or emotional energy to take on anything new or difficult.

Suddenly, with Josh's proposal, an escape had been offered to her. The most important thing now was to look ahead, instead of dwelling on the past. And a proposal of marriage was, above all, a vision of the future.

Josh had already proved himself to be strong and protective, yet, compared to her, he seemed pleasantly weak. She was attracted to him more than anything by the fact that his physical strength – his large, powerful body – somehow carried with it not an ounce of threat. Through someone like Josh, she could feel protected without ever feeling exposed, as she was with Guy. He was utterly loyal, and he seemed to love her with a certainty she had never before witnessed in anyone. He needed her. He would never betray her or give up on her. Already, she felt as if he belonged to her.

All she had to do was tell him that she had accepted him, and a new, safe chapter of her life would be opened. His muscle, his presence would be added to hers. Through him, she would feel stronger, bigger and tougher. Josh, perhaps, after all the injustice, was her reward. With him, life would at long last get easier.

Moreover, marriage was the perfect revenge on Guy. It was the best way possible to demonstrate that she had left him behind – that she had moved on – that he was no longer the dominant influence on her life. Guy had been suspicious of Josh for a long time. If she married him – and married him quickly – this would represent a victory. Guy would be left feeling that Lisa had emerged with the very thing she wanted all along. He might even suspect that she had cheated on him before he cheated on her. Whatever he concluded, he certainly wouldn't be able to pity or patronize her. He would know for sure that she had come out on top.

Also, her period was a week late.

'OK,' she says. 'All right. I'll marry you.'

37

Graham and Keri emerge from the cinema feeling, more than anything else, confused. They wander down the street in bewildered silence.

'Those films are amazing,' he says.

'Why?'

'You know – the credits are probably still rolling, we've walked thirty seconds down the street, and I know I enjoyed myself, but I can't remember what we just saw.'

'That's true, actually,' she says.

'What *did* we just see?'

'I don't know. We did just see a film, didn't we?'

Graham stops walking and scrabbles in his pockets, eventually fishing out a crumpled cinema ticket. He unravels it and peers at the various numbers printed across its wrinkly surface. 'It's got today's date on it,' he says, narrowing his eyes and attempting to impersonate a hyper-intelligent voice.

'It's been torn in half,' Keri adds, coming over all *X-Files*. 'That would indicate that we did go into the cinema.'

'How do we know the projector was working?' he says.

'Do you feel like you've been asleep?'

'No.'

'And you weren't bored?'

'No.'

'So they must have shown us *something*,' she says.

'A film?'

'Maybe.'

'Or something else . . .'

Keri squeezes his arm, as if petrified, her mouth gaping open, then she suddenly gets bored and demands that they go for a drink.

They walk around the West End, poking their heads into various pubs, all of which seem to be suffering rather badly from Friday-night syndrome – huge gangs of pissed men in suits screaming at each other over deafening music, with a few shivering people stubbornly attempting to hold a conversation outside on the pavement, standing in a thin scattering of broken glass.

Deciding they are both feeling too hyper for a café, they resolve to accept the next pub that comes, however unpleasant it is.

Soon finding one that resembles all the others, they hover outside and listen to the muffled din. They smile at one another, take a deep breath, and barge in. Wading through a thick fog of noise, smoke and sweat, the pair of them stake out a corner.

'We've got somewhere for our drinks,' shouts Keri, tapping a soggy, narrow fake mahogany shelf, screwed into the wall at elbow height.

'Luxury!' says Graham. 'It's like the Ritz.'

'Only more sedate.'

'What?'

'More sedate. More fucking sedate.'

'Right. Exactly. Beer?'

She nods, and Graham pushes through the crowd to the bar.

Returning to their spot he finds Keri gone, replaced by a group of three weird-looking Soho types who are either extremely trendy or taking the piss or both. Turning his head, he spots a waving hand and picks out Keri standing by the farthest wall at the back of the pub. He inches his way towards her.

'Quieter here,' she says.

'Is it?'

'Not under a speaker.'

He shrugs and places a pint in her hand. She takes a big gulp, then puts her drink down on a nearby table. She smirks at him, takes the other pint from his hand, which he still hasn't touched, and deposits it next to hers. Graham frowns at her, confused. She steps forward and gives him a long, slow kiss on the lips.

She then steps back again, picks up his drink, puts it in his hand, picks up her drink, takes a swig, and smiles at him as if nothing has happened.

Graham, meanwhile, is frozen to the spot.

'This tastes funny,' she says, puckering her mouth.

Graham's jaw creeps open. 'Did you . . . ?'

'Mmm,' she says. 'Sorry. I've been wanting to do that for ages.'

His limbs still frozen, Graham begins to sway slightly, as if he has just been punched in the face. Shuffling to regain his balance, he squints at Keri, flabbergasted.

'How come?' he says, eventually.

'I felt like it.'

'How come?' he repeats, after a long silence, seemingly unaware that he has just asked the same question.

'I just did. Don't you?'

'Me? Me?' He splutters a laugh, shaking his head. 'Actually, no. I don't believe in sexual contact with fantastically beautiful women.'

'You don't?'

'No. It's against my principles. In fact, there's nothing worse than being kissed out of the blue by a woman you've been dreaming about and lusting after for weeks on end.'

'Really?' says Keri, a grin spreading across her face. Relief and excitement suddenly tingle in her veins. She's got him. He's not a eunuch, after all. Just a coward. 'Nothing worse?'

'I'm in shock.'

'It must have been awful for you.'

'I can't describe it. I'm going to have nightmares now about . . . about tearing your clothes off and licking you all over, and . . .'

'I don't think I want to be licked all over.'

'Maybe not *all* over. Some bits more than others.'

She really has got him. A proper man. Someone who can laugh at himself. 'Which bits in particular?' she says, with a level gaze.

Graham, thrown by the turn the conversation has taken, moves his pint from hand to hand, exercising his fingers in an attempt to try and dispel the strange numbness which seems to have crept over his body. 'The . . . er . . . I reckon the soles of your feet would be a good start,' he says, a comment which in his head sounded cool and flirtatious, but which somehow comes out as beseeching and pathetic.

Keri groans with mock-revulsion, then gives Graham another fat kiss on the mouth. He takes it with significantly improved composure, this time looking less punch-drunk, more like the recipient of a mild electric shock.

He earths himself against the wall, steadying his balance, before asking, 'Are you . . . taking the piss or something?'

'What do you mean?'

'This isn't – like – a joke.'

'What isn't a joke?'

'You. Do you – I mean – like me?'

'Yes.'

'You fancy me?'

'Of course I do.'

'Physically?'

'*Yes!*'

'Really? You're not joking?'

'For God's sake, Graham – why do you think I've been spending all this time with you?'

'I don't know. I thought we were mates.'

'We are mates.'

'Except that you fancy me?'

'Yes,' she says, with a nod.

'Physically?'

'Yes, physically. Why do you keep saying that?'

'I don't know. It's just weird. I can't really believe it. Are you sure?'

'Of course I'm sure. What's your problem?'

'I don't know.'

'Do you not fancy me?'

'Don't say that,' he snaps.

'Why?'

'It's an insult.'

'To what?'

'To me. To my . . . I mean . . . I don't *fancy* you. That's totally the wrong word. I . . . you're . . . perfect. You're amazingly beautiful and you're a good laugh and we really get on and you're just . . . I mean . . . even just being your friend, I love you. If I never got to lay a finger on you, I'd still love you.'

Graham's eyes flick away from Keri and glance nervously around the room.

She sips her drink, watching him fidget. He is exhibiting all the over-keenness and desperation which usually make her flee for her life, but somehow, coming from Graham, it all seems endearing. Nothing is concealed or disguised. There is no ego twisting his awkwardness into aggression or coldness. He wouldn't have a clue how to play power games even if he wanted to. He can't even hide the fact that he panics when she touches him. He's an idiot, and she loves him for it.

She smiles, feeling a momentary twinge in her clitoris, like a ring on a hotel receptionist's bell.

'What do we do now?' he says.

Keri raises an eyebrow. 'What do you think?'

'Are you talking . . . like . . . consummation?'

She shrugs. 'That sort of area.'

'Right. Wow. This is so weird.' Graham's face begins to lose its colour, and beer begins sloshing around his glass, a few dribbles slipping out over his trembling hands.

'I need to sit down.'

'What's wrong?'

'I just . . . fuck . . . this whole thing's freaking me out. I never thought this would happen. I . . . you know . . . I've never felt like this about anyone before and it's all having a very weird effect on me and the thought of actually being in bed with you is just so mad that I just . . . I mean . . . I don't know what kind of effect this whole emotional thing has on male blood-circulation but my hands are going cold just thinking about it, so I almost certainly won't be able to . . . you know . . . the whole thing might be a disaster.'

'You think that's likely?'

'I'm just saying – if things go wrong, it's not for lack of enthusiasm on my part. I just – you know – can't legislate for what might happen. My body's going to think I've died and gone to heaven, and I don't reckon they have erections in heaven.'

'I think there are probably lots of erections in heaven. On demand. Big ones.'

'There ought to be. But what if there aren't?'

'We'll just have to do an experiment. Make a private little heaven together and see if I can coax one out of you.'

'OK. Good idea,' he says, almost swallowing his tongue. 'It's got to be worth a try.'

'I think so.'

'Sounds like a *very* good experiment. Maybe we can get government funding.'

'And publish the results.'

'Assuming we don't spill them.'

Keri laughs, and an odd silence descends as they each take a gulp of beer.

'All I was trying to say is,' Graham adds, 'because I – you know – like you so much more than usual, it's not – physiologically – a position I've been in before. And you took me by surprise. So I'm just a bit freaked out.'

'I noticed.'

'I'm not a weirdo, or anything.'

'Of course not.'

'I talk a lot of shit, but I'm – you know – OK.'

'Graham?'

'Yeah.'

Keri holds a pause, staring into his eyes. 'Stop talking.'

'OK.'

'I understand.'

'OK.'

'You don't have to worry.'

'I'm not worried. I might faint, but it's not because I'm worried.'

'Good.'

'Good.'

'So let's go,' she says. 'This place is nasty.'

'Go?' he says.

'Yes.'

'Home?'

'Yes.'

'OK.'

He nods and stares at her, not moving.

'Now?' she says.

'Good idea. Right. You want to go home?'

'Yeah.'

'Can I come with you?'

Keri laughs and hits him on the arm. 'Don't be such an idiot.'

'Just checking. You can't be too careful. It's very

hard to tell what women are thinking, you know.'

'Yeah, right.'

'I don't want you to think I'm molesting you.'

'That's *exactly* what I've been thinking. You're so pushy, Graham.'

'You know how it is. A man like me. Impossible to resist. Women are helpless.'

'Totally.' Keri kisses him again – their third kiss – and for the first time, Graham seems to enjoy it. Hand in hand, she leads him through the crush of bodies and out into the street.

38

Guy has only one piece of mail: a postcard, face up on the doormat, showing an image of luminous blue sea backing on to high cliffs, with a small white-domed church perched amongst the topmost rocks, overlooking the water. On a white band across the bottom of the card a caption says, 'The Beautiful Island of Amorgos'. Guy turns it over, and immediately recognizes Helen's handwriting.

Trembling now, he has to move the card close to his face and hold it in both hands to steady it for reading.

> *Dear Guy,*
>
> *Sorry I haven't been in touch. I'm fine and am having a good time. I hope you haven't been worried about me. Things were a little strange for a while and I left in rather a rush, but everything is OK now and I am hoping to see you soon.*
>
> *love,*
>
> *Helen*
>
> *xxxx*

Motionless, Guy reads these four sentences over and over again, until he knows them by heart. The stamp is Greek, but there is no return address, or any further information about where Helen might be. The post-mark, although smudged and in an alien alphabet, seems to bear the same place name as the front of the card.

Guy rushes to the phone and rings Helen's parents.

'Hi. It's Guy. I – . . .'

'We're packing,' says Helen's mother.

'What?'

'We're packing. I can't talk. We got a card this morning. We think we know where she is.'

'This morning?'

'Yes. I really can't talk. We think she's OK. The travel agent's calling us back in a minute.'

'So did I,' says Guy.

'What?'

'So did I. I got a card. This morning. From Helen.'

'You got a card?'

'Yes.'

'From Greece?'

'Yes.'

'Oh, my God. *He got a card! He got one, too. It's Guy! Also from Greece!* What does it say? What . . . ? Is she all right? Read it to me. *Come to the phone. Come to the phone. He's going to read it.* Wait a minute. OK. OK. Read it.'

Guy reads his card to the two parents, audibly huddled around a single receiver. There is a silence on the other end of the line, so Guy reads it again.

249

Another silence follows, then he hears a conversation start between them.

'It's the same,' the mother says, sounding bemused and flat.

'It's the same thing,' says Helen's father, his words distant and hollow. This is the first time Guy has ever heard his voice – an observation which flashes through Guy with a throat-tightening stab of sympathy. There is something inhumane in this proximity to the misery and confusion of strangers. He doesn't know this man – he has never seen him and has never before heard him speak – yet Guy's words have such awful power over him.

Helen's parents continue to stammer at one another, neither voice near the receiver of the telephone.

'What does that mean?'

'Every word,' says the father.

'What does that mean?'

'Is that bad?'

'Word for word.'

'Is that bad?'

'I don't know. I don't know.'

They fall silent.

'Hello?' says Guy. 'What is it?'

'It's the same,' says Helen's mother, coming back on the line. 'The one we got was exactly the same. Every word. "Sorry I haven't been in touch. I'm fine and am having a good time."' She quotes with cold speed, clearly from memory, her tone of voice imbuing Helen's words with a sinister insincerity. ' "I hope you haven't been worried about me. Things were a little strange for a while and I left in rather a rush, but everything is OK now and I am hoping to see you both soon. Love, Helen." It's the same. There's a "both" at the end of ours, but other than that every word is the same.'

'What does that mean?' says Guy.

'I don't know. I don't know,' she repeats.

'It's strange. Why would she do that?'

'It doesn't have to be bad,' she says. 'It might not be bad. It might not mean anything.'

'It probably doesn't mean anything. She just picked what she wanted to say. It doesn't . . . I mean, it's no reason to think she's not OK. If she says she's OK, she must be OK.'

'Yes. She must be OK. Or she wouldn't have written.'

'Exactly,' he says. 'Exactly.'

'She waited long enough, and now she's all right. She must be all right.'

'And you're going to find her?' says Guy.

'Yes. We're flying to Athens. We've looked on the map. It's not a big island. If she's still there, we can probably find her. We think she didn't write before because she didn't want to be found. Once it had been long enough to make us worried, she knew that if she wrote, we'd go and look for her, so she didn't write while she didn't want to see anyone. That's why she didn't write. And now she has, which means she wants us to go. And we want to see her. We want to be sure she's OK, and tell her she can come back whenever she wants. That's what the card means. She's gone out of her way to let us know where she is. She doesn't want to make anyone go and get her, but we think she wouldn't have written if she still wanted to be alone.'

'I'll go,' says Guy, suddenly. He doesn't know where the words come from. He just says them.

'What?'

'I'll go. If . . . I mean . . . The panic's over. We know she's OK. And she might not even be there any more. But if she is, it means she wants to see someone – which is what you're saying. And if it's a friend, rather than . . . you know . . . her parents, it might be easier for her. She wrote to me, too. There must be a reason for that. And she might get in touch again. She might phone you. Someone should stay behind and see if she sends any more news. She might be moving around. I can head out there, and if she sends another card from somewhere else, I can follow her. She might be hard to find. I can call you each day to say if there's any news. And we know she's OK. It's the best plan. I want to go. You can trust me. I promise.'

'I don't know . . .'

'It's a good idea. It makes much better sense. Going there would . . . if it proves frustrating, it could make things much worse for you. If it's only me . . . it just makes more sense.'

'We'll have to think about it.'

'Of course.'

'Give us a while. We'll talk it through.'

'I think it's a good idea.'

'You're right that someone should stay behind.'

'It's important. And we don't know what happened. There must be a reason why she left. I can talk to her. If it's just me it might be less . . . you know.'

'We'll call you back.'

'I can go. I want to go. I can give a message from you. Or deliver a letter. I can get her to phone you.'

'We'll call you back in a minute.'

'OK.'

'We'll call you back.'

'OK.'

39

Hand in hand with Graham, walking out of Tower
Records (where he has just bought two bossa nova
collections, a Public Enemy album and the *Best of
Steely Dan*), Keri suddenly stops dead. Immediately
in front of her, with her back turned, buying an
Evening Standard, is Lisa.

Keri freezes, unsure what to do, then Lisa turns
round and they catch one another's eye.

Lisa pauses for a moment, blanches, then turns
her head towards the traffic and walks away, down
Piccadilly. Without thinking, Keri chases after her.

'Lisa! Lisa!'

Keri touches Lisa's arm, which is instantly yanked
away. After a few more hurried steps, Keri still following and calling after her, Lisa suddenly stops dead and
spins round, her face clenched with hatred. 'What?
What do you want?'

'I just . . . I don't know . . . I haven't seen you.'

'And now you have.'

'There's a lot to say.'

'There's nothing to say.'

'I . . . look . . . this is the wrong place to have
this conversation, but I'm really sorry about what
happened. I really am sorry. I feel awful and I don't

know why I did it and . . . and I know you must hate me and I understand if you don't want to see me, but if you ever do, I'd really like to . . . to see you again. I miss you, and – . . .'

'Fuck you. You don't understand anything.'

'Well . . . I'm sorry that's how you feel. If you can't . . . if you don't want to forgive me, that's . . . that's your right.'

'Don't tell me what my rights are.'

'I'm not. I just . . . I can't tell you how much I regret what we did. I just want you to know I'm sorry. And I can see you don't accept it, but if you ever do, I'll be . . . I mean . . . I'd like to see you again. I really would.'

'You think I'll be dropping round for a coffee?'

'Lisa – . . .'

'Don't patronize me.'

'I'm not. Look. We should talk another time.'

'I'm not interested. There's nothing to say.'

Keri stares at Lisa, incredulous that their years of friendship have reached such a definitive full stop. She feels weak with guilt, her mind fumbling for a means to communicate the sincerity of her feelings – for a way of expressing a genuine humility that might get through Lisa's anger.

From her posture, Keri can see that Lisa is on the verge of walking away again. Keri has to say something – anything – just to prolong the conversation.

'And . . . congratulations,' she says, 'on . . . on . . . I mean I heard about the engagement and everything. I hope . . . you know . . . well done and everything.'

'That's big of you.'

'I mean it.'

'I don't care what you mean and what you don't mean, Keri. I don't give a shit any more. You're nothing. You're no one. You understand that? I don't need your insincere, mealy-mouthed . . . in fact, I really don't want to hear anything you've got to say about my fucking engagement, because I know you don't mean a fucking word of it, and I've had enough of your lying shit over the years, and to be honest, I'm glad I don't have to put up with it any more. I know what you think. I know what you really think. I know what you think about me, and I certainly know what you think about him. OK? So don't fucking patronize me. I haven't forgotten. And he is worth so much more than you or anyone like you. You know that? What you did to him is exactly the same thing you did to me. You don't understand that and you never will, but it's true. And I don't have time for that in my life any more. I've grown out of that. I don't have space for people like you. I've pulled myself out of the shit – and I've got away from all your vain, insincere, selfish crap, and I really never want to see you or Guy or anyone like you ever again. OK? And I certainly don't want to hear your fucking opinions on my fucking marriage. All right?'

Keri stares at Lisa, trembling, lost for words.

'You with him, now?' says Lisa, nodding towards Graham, who is hovering awkwardly behind Keri.

Keri turns to Graham, then back to Lisa, and nods.

'Hah!' snaps Lisa, a dry and sarcastic bark. 'You deserve each other.'

And with that, Lisa walks on, against the flow of pedestrians, soon disappearing into the crowd of advancing faces.

Graham puts an arm round Keri, whose body is rigid, her face frozen, staring at the spot where Lisa was standing.

'You OK?' he says.

Keri's face suddenly crumples, and she begins to sob into Graham's shoulder, harder and louder as he pulls her tighter against him.

He holds her close, losing all sense of passing time, and when she has calmed to a few quiet snuffles, he nestles his face against her wet cheek and whispers in her ear, 'I always liked Lisa. Great sense of humour.'

Keri laughs, a bubble of snot bursting on the end of her nose.

'Please,' he says, softly. 'Spray me with bogeys. I love it.'

Keri pulls a wet-faced puffy smile, wiping her top lip with a sleeve.

'She's right, you know,' says Graham, hugging her again. 'We do deserve each other. I'm your punishment for sleeping with Guy. I'm your penance, sent from above.'

'What about me, then?'

'You're my reward for fifteen years of selfless charity work in the soup kitchens of Calcutta.'

'You haven't done fifteen years' charity work.'

'I know. God obviously thinks I have, though. I reckon it was a clerical error.'

'What – you're my punishment and I'm your clerical error?'

'Something like that,' he says, folding her cold, delicate fingers into the warmth of his palms.

Keri looks at him, through her swollen and raw eyes, seeing his face more clearly than she has ever seen it before. She holds his gaze, and they stare at each other, unsmiling, two motionless bodies impeding the flow on a busy London pavement, both suddenly gripped by the silent, intense upswell of an unreserved mutual acceptance, blessing their look and their touch with an electricity of trust and anticipation.

Almost crying again, her throat beginning to tighten, Keri breaks the moment with a smile and a slow, deep kiss.

'Well,' she says, sucking in a tiny blob of saliva from her bottom lip, 'I'm glad there's an angel up there who's a bad typist.'

Graham kisses her once more, gently, on the mouth.

'Me too,' he says. 'Me too.'

40

The sleek, white Skopelitis Lines ferry steadied itself as it entered the horseshoe of flat, blue water surrounding the port of Katapola. As the boat turned into calmer sea, Guy's shade slid away, the low sun hitting him full in the face. Tossing his sun-wrinkled novel aside, Guy stood and leaned against the iron deck-side railing. Fumbling his sunglasses down from the top of his head, he watched Katapola swing into view, his heartbeat accelerating with the mingled thrill and fear of arrival.

A row of white box houses, all with identical blue shutters, were spread round the small bay with a sweet uniformity somehow reminiscent of dressed-up children arrayed for a school photo. The land rose sharply from the sea into an arc of dry, craggy mountains, and in only a few spots did the houses sit uphill from the sea front. Every building was the same two-tone blue and white, all of them simple cubes except for the town's two churches, which singled themselves out with modest blue domes.

If this was the full extent of the main port on the island – and if Helen was still here – it wouldn't take long to find her. Beginning to ponder how he would set about his search, an odd reluctance tugged at Guy's conscience. Almost jealously, he sensed the calm and space of this isolated spot as an invitation to relax, and to find out what was really going on in his own head. After only two days in Greece, he already saw with new clarity the extent of his failure to come to terms with the loss of Lisa. Away from London, he could feel his mind unravelling. No specific ideas or revelations had come to him – he simply sensed his mental canvas expanding.

However concerned he was for Helen's welfare, however eager he was to see her, he couldn't help feeling reluctant to sacrifice his solitude. He wanted Helen to be safe, but a part of him guiltily hoped she would prove hard to find. A week on his own, looking for her, would be perfect.

The ferry hooted its arrival and noisily dropped anchor, delicately swinging its giant rear towards a small concrete pontoon which constituted the island's one physical link to the outside world. Within minutes of the drawbridge hitting land, the single road around the bay was buzzing with cars, motorbikes, vans and scooters. Half an hour later, the island was quiet again – Guy surveying the peace from the top-floor window of a small pension on the far side of the bay.

He had been intending to come directly to Amorgos, but for the lack of a direct ferry he had been forced ashore at Naxos. Away from the cloying panic of Helen's parents, Guy felt certain that she was alive and physically healthy. She would probably be an emotional wreck, though, and nervous of what would be required of him when he found her, Guy took a couple of days on Naxos to prepare himself. He felt he needed a holiday of his own before confronting – as ever – problems which seemed to belong more to other people than to him. He knew, somehow, that he would find her. She wouldn't have sent the postcard if she didn't want to be found. She wasn't a tease. The postcard, as her parents in their garbled way had realized, was Helen's signal that she was ready to give an explanation for her disappearance to someone who was willing to go and get it.

The fact that she had issued this invitation after such a long gap, however, filled Guy with dread. Helen had an enormous capacity for misery. No one had spoken to her for a full three months. She could be in any condition, and there was little ground for optimism.

Guy's pension had a small taverna attached – a few rickety chairs spilling out towards the seashore – where Guy sat by candlelight, drinking, awaiting the arrival of his moussaka. The row of restaurants on the far side of the water, near the ferry port, glowed across the water, shimmering in reflection, giving out a just-perceptible buzz of conversation and music – at this volume, somehow a perfect accompaniment to the timid lapping of docile sea on a shingle beach.

Guy took a swig of beer, its tart chill sinking deliciously into his hot chest, and felt a swell of happiness glow inside him. This was right. He was in the right place. This was what it felt like to be happy. Only now, recognizing the unfamiliarity of this sensation, did it dawn on him that for months – as much during the build-up to his split with Lisa as in its aftermath – he had been miserable. Their relationship had soured long before anything came to the surface. The whole process had extracted a long, gloomy chunk from his year.

Now the rise and fall of pain was at last, it seemed, finishing. Lisa was easing her way out of his brain. The thoughts which had been chasing themselves around his head in the last weeks were gradually beginning to seem less circular. After a few days of clear thought, his resentments and annoyances began to feel irrelevant. In various ways they had let one another down, and these petty betrayals, for the first time, failed to irk him. Their break-up had happened – it wasn't still happening.

Away from London, away from the flat he had shared with her for so long, away from Graham's perennially bad advice, he could feel the blizzard of events settling. There was nothing he had to do or say to deal with it – he just had to think. Only now, only here, did thought really seem possible. For months, he realized, he had been worrying, fretting and niggling at his problems, but not thinking.

The heat, the stretch of open water in front of him, the cool beer, the food on the way to his table – this was what he needed to find the right kind of thought. It wasn't the kind of thinking you could *do*. It wasn't quite active; nor was it passive. It didn't contain flashes of inspiration, or even any real ideas. A breeze was passing through his brain, gently shifting aside the clutter in its path. Guy's mind was clearing, leaving behind the peace you acquire as you become bored by your own problems.

The following morning, finishing off a perfect breakfast of yoghurt with honey, melon and grapes at one of the bayside cafés, Guy spots a familiar figure.

Beyond a sea of chairs, perhaps three or four restaurants down, Helen, tanned and thin, in a figure-hugging T-shirt, is carrying a heavily laden tray at shoulder height with balanced ease. Wearing an efficient smile, she deposits various bowls, plates and mugs around the terrace, pausing to share a somehow foreign-language-looking joke with a couple under the parasol nearest to the sea. Then, with a last comment over her shoulder, she spins the empty tray down to her side and swiftly disappears back inside.

Guy's first thought on seeing her is mild surprise that she has such a good body. This settles and departs like a housefly, displaced almost immediately by a huge wave of relief. She is OK. She even looks happy.

Guy watches her rush in and out of the restaurant,

taking orders and bringing food, his heart quickening a fraction each time she emerges into view. He had entirely forgotten, amidst all the worry about her well-being, how much he missed her.

When the number of breakfasting customers has died down, he walks to her restaurant and quietly takes a seat facing away from the kitchens, looking out towards the sea. That way he will be able to see her full reaction. She won't have a chance to recognize him until she is standing right at his table.

A few seconds later she is there, standing over him, smiling. She barely does a double-take when she sees him. A quick blink of surprise, immediately followed by a grin and a kiss on the cheek is all he gets.

'I was hoping it would be you,' she says.

'Well it is.'

Somehow this reunion already feels like something of an anticlimax. Helen doesn't seem relieved or even particularly delighted to see him.

'I'm glad it's not Mum and Dad,' she says.

'So am I.'

Smiling at her like an idiot, squinting into the sun, his neck craned upwards, Guy is amazed to find himself at a loss for words.

'Can you talk?' he says eventually, nodding towards the restaurant.

She shrugs and shakes her head. 'Not really. Not now.'

'Can you take the day off?'

'Tomorrow, maybe. I'll ask.'

'OK.'

'Thank you for coming,' she says, putting a hand on his shoulder and kissing him again on the cheek – an almost patronizing gesture which makes Guy feel unexpectedly strange. Their roles seem to be not at all what he had anticipated. He feels almost embarrassed – as if he is the supplicant – not at all Helen's long-awaited saviour from back home. He feels like a guest. A welcome guest, but awkwardly so: an idle visitor in a busy home.

'What do you want?' she says.

'Eh?' Guy flushes, confused – her question clicking bizarrely and offensively into place with his thought process.

'To eat,' says Helen.

'Oh, right. OK. Er . . . I've eaten. Just a coffee.'

'OK. Have a *café frappe*. It's what the Greeks have. It's better in the heat.'

'All right. Don't know what it is, but I'll have it.'

'It's iced. Milk and sugar?'

'Yeah.'

'I'll ask about tomorrow.'

'Cool.'

Guy sits awkwardly at his table for a far longer time than it can possibly take to make one coffee before Helen emerges, laughing, from the restaurant, carrying a tall brown drink, most of which appears to be froth. She places it on the table in front of him, deftly slipping a paper napkin under the glass with a practised flick of the fingers. She is still smiling.

'They think you're my boyfriend,' she says. 'They said I don't need the day off – I have to take the night off instead.'

'Oh,' says Guy, embarrassed.

Helen laughs again, this time at Guy's reaction. 'They're taking the piss, Guy. Katerina says she'll get her sister to cover for me. I've been on a seven-day week for the whole month. It should be fine.'

'Good.'

'What do you want to do?'

'Dunno,' says Guy. 'Talk. Catch up.'

'Walk?' says Helen.

'OK.'

'There's a church on a headland at the top of the island. I've been meaning to go for ages. It's supposed to be beautiful.'

'OK.'

'I'll meet you at the bus stand at ten. I have to work tonight. I'm really sorry. It's mad at the moment. You've come right in the middle of high season.'

'It's fine,' he says with a forced smile. 'I didn't realize you'd have a job, but I suppose it's obvious, really.'

'What did you think I was doing? What am I supposed to live off?'

'Don't know. It just hadn't occurred to me.'

'We've got the whole day tomorrow.'

'It's fine. I'm being stupid. Where's this bus place?'

'Just there,' she says, pointing. 'Right where the ferry docks.'

'OK. Ten.'

'You've got somewhere to stay?' says Helen.

'Yeah. It's fine.'

'I'd invite you, but I'm in a tiny . . .'

'My place is fine. Don't worry.'

Helen hovers over him, sensing Guy's awkwardness. She doesn't quite feel she can go back to work.

'It's funny,' he says, smiling at her diffidently.

'What?' Helen glances out to sea, pushing a strand of hair away from her face.

'This,' he says. 'It's not what I expected. You seem fine.'

'I am fine.'

'We all thought something had happened.'

Helen shrugs. Guy scrutinizes her face.

'What are you doing here?' he says.

Helen eyes him squarely. 'Waitressing,' she replies. 'Why?'

She doesn't answer.

'Why didn't you tell anyone you were going?'

'I can't talk now, Guy. I'm sorry.'

Guy shrugs at her, frowning.

'Tomorrow,' she says.

'Ten. Bus stop.'

She nods and takes a step back from his table, tapping a thigh with her empty tray.

'Don't work too hard,' he adds.

She smiles and walks away.

'I'll tell you if this is nice!' he calls after her, holding up his drink.

She lifts a hand in acknowledgement and disappears into the restaurant.

41

The bus rises sharply on a series of hairpin bends out of Katapola's bay. As a view over the valley, town and sea swings in and out of view, expanding with each pass, Helen and Guy gaze out in concentrated, appreciative silence. For half an hour they growl along a high ridge blasted out of the mountainside, with a vast, radiant blueness filling all the windows along one side of the bus. Helen seems lost in the view – or at least keen to give the impression that she is – and when Guy catches her eye, she simply smiles at him, saying nothing, before looking back out to sea.

As they pull into Eyiali, the northern town on the island, Guy suggests stopping for a drink but Helen hurries him into a shop, saying that they have to get going before the worst of the day's heat. She buys a couple of nectarines, a bottle of water and a pack of biscuits, exchanging a few words with the shopkeeper in Greek. She even disputes her change, somehow making the shopkeeper laugh in the process.

'What did you say to him?' says Guy, as they leave the shop.

'He gave me a torn banknote. I handed it back and told him to give it to a tourist.'

'Since when do you speak Greek?'

'I don't. I'm just starting.'

'Sounds pretty fluent to me.'

'Nowhere near.'

'Still – in three months . . .'

'You pick it up quickly if you hang around with Greeks. I've got a good ear for it.'

'You must have,' says Guy, trying not to display his shock at her self-assured, almost arrogant turn of phrase.

Helen asks a few passers-by for directions to the footpath, unsuccessfully, until an old man points them in the right direction, squeezing his legs with an encouraging laugh and telling them it is a long way.

As soon as they have found it – a jagged, stony path climbing slowly under an imposing grey escarpment, enclosed on either side by orangey-brown dry-stone walls, Helen strides out. Guy has to struggle to keep up, and only manages to do so at a consistent half-stride behind her.

'How did you get your job?' he says, breathlessly.

'Just turned up.'

'How?'

'I was drinking there one lunchtime, and they were really overworked – it's just an old married couple that run the place – they're a bit doddery – and these stupid English people were making a huge fuss about something being too cold or too slow, and I just started helping. I helped them all afternoon, and all evening, then I just came back the next day. It seemed like the obvious thing to do.'

'They pay you?'

'Sort of. I eat what I want. They gave me a room in their house. I make up to ten quid a day in tips. It's plenty for round here.'

'When did this happen?'

'Week or two after I left England.'

'You've been in that restaurant for three months?'

'Almost. I sorted the whole place out for them. I did English and French menus. I went over to Naxos with Katerina and traded in their old wooden chairs for some nice canvas ones. I persuaded them to replace the parasols. We've got new tables coming next week. Funny thing is, everyone's more overworked now than when I got there. They're making money, though. It's really good, Guy. I've made a big difference.'

'And it's fun?'

'Not exactly. It's hard work. But I think maybe work is more fun than fun. It's satisfying. Feeding people.'

'Being a waitress?'

'I'm more than that. Everyone does everything. I'm part of the business. I've put them into profit.'

'And all you get is bed and board?'

'They treat me like a daughter.'

'You mean they underpay you.'

'It's not like that,' she says heavily, breaking her

stride to stare at Guy. 'It isn't. I've really found something here.'

'Sorry.'

'I'm happy,' she says, an edge of defiance in her
voice.

'I can tell.'

Helen turns and strides on. Guy struggles to catch
up, then, sensing that a little silence is required, he
relaxes and falls into step with her, no longer trying
to keep up, simply following her rhythm, one pace
behind, admiring the rise and fall of her backside as
she presses on up the mountain.

When they stop for water, Helen doesn't remove her
sunglasses, and without being able to form proper eye
contact, Guy finds it hard to talk to her. She doesn't
seem to be looking at him properly.

'Can I ask?' he says, eventually.

'What?'

'If everything was so fine, why didn't you tell anyone where you were?'

'I didn't say everything *was* fine. I just said it's fine
now.'

'What was wrong?'

'I just wanted to be on my own,' she says, with a
definitiveness that stalls the conversation. Everything
in her body language and her tone of voice seems to
imply resentment at Guy's presence. Something in her
manner has made him afraid of her.

'Do you still want to be on your own?' he says, his heart pounding.

Helen removes her sunglasses.

'No,' she says, after a long silence. Her voice softens, and she holds his gaze for the first time that day. 'No,' she repeats, an awkward smile teasing the edges of her mouth.

The perpetual chorus of rasping crickets seems to fill the air entirely, blotting out the speechlessness between them. Guy exhales and looks away, more relieved than he dares show. A moment of contact, at last, has been reached.

Guy looks at the town, now way below them, the tiny houses like a scatter of Scrabble pieces, sensing for the first time that perhaps, after all, he is a welcome visitor. The knot in his chest, whose presence he has hitherto not even acknowledged to himself, can maybe now begin to loosen.

'Sorry if I've been a bit cold,' she says.

'It's OK,' Guy replies, turning to look at her. 'If it's how you feel . . .'

'It's not how I feel. I'm just . . . nervous, that's all.'

'About what?'

She thinks, looking up at the rock-face above them and the parched brown fields on either side of the path.

'Can we just walk?' she says, eventually.

'OK. If you want. Walk, though. Not sprint.'

She laughs. 'Have I been going a bit fast?'

'No – I love triathlons. We are swimming home, aren't we?'

'Sorry. It's waitressing. Keeps you fit.'

They set off again, this time more slowly, side by side, in a silence which somehow stretches out comfortably between them, increasingly relaxed and companionable as the rising sun slowly makes them hotter, sweatier and more loose-limbed. For the first time since his arrival, Guy feels confident that Helen wants him there. As the walk progresses, the fact that she doesn't yet want to talk openly with him seems like less and less of a problem. The important thing is simply spending time with her. What they say to one another, oddly, feels secondary.

At midday they stop under a spindly pine tree and remove their backpacks. Their faces are shiny with a coating of sweat, and they both have a wet line around each shoulder from the straps of their bags. The coast is now hidden from view behind them, and they are in a wide, dry ridge between two adjacent peaks. A few fields, terraced into the side of the valley with crumbling stone walls, spread below the path, dotted with the odd olive tree and a few parched vines.

They listen in happy silence to the rasp of the crickets and the occasional jangle of a goat bell from the higher slopes, each eating a nectarine and swigging water, before Guy says, 'You don't know what happened to me.'

Helen frowns at him, curious, and for the next hour, each sitting on their own shaded rock in the heavy, humid, pine-scented air, Guy describes the collapse of his relationship with Lisa. It is the first time he has told the entire story from beginning to end, and this process of giving the confusing jumble of events a narrative shape immediately clarifies Guy's thoughts. He is surprised to find how easily he can relate what happened. The sequence of emotions, he discovers, does make sense. It is a story now, with an ending. He can arrive at a natural finish without tailing off into uncertainties about what might happen or what he wants to happen or what he might end up doing. The story simply concludes with the fact that they are apart, and will stay apart. He can think and even say this without an electric circuit of hopes and fears sparking to life in his brain. He is at last, he realizes, free of her.

At the end of his description, Helen leaves a long silence before saying, simply, 'You did the right thing.'

'I did the right thing?' he replies, amazed. 'I did an awful thing.'

'OK. You didn't *do* the right thing – but the result is the right result.'

'Why?'

'It just is.'

'Why?'

'You held each other back. You didn't love each other.'

'How can you know that?'

'It was obvious.'

'You can't tell what goes on in private, Helen. Our relationship wasn't so bad.'

'It wasn't good.'

'You don't know that.'

'I do. I know you.'

'And?'

'You did what you did for a reason.'

'What reason?'

'I don't know. Desperation.'

'How do you know I'm not just a bastard?'

'That's what I'm saying. That's all I do know.'

'What?'

'That you're not a bastard. That you wouldn't have done it unless you had to. You wouldn't have done it if you loved her.'

'I wish I could believe that. I don't think I can let myself off the hook so easily.'

'I didn't say you're off the hook,' says Helen, with a tiny smile. 'You're still on the hook. You did a bad thing. But you did it because you don't love her, which means you're both better off out of the relationship.'

'What happened to female solidarity? Why aren't you pulling my hair and telling me I'm a typical male git?'

'Hmph.'

'What does that mean?'

'Me and Lisa. You know . . .'

'What? Hated each other?'

'Basically. That's what happened to female solidarity. She's bad news. You were always too good for her.'

'This is what I need to hear.'

'Even if you are a typical male git,' she adds.

Guy laughs. 'You promise you don't think badly of me,' he says, after a pause. 'For what I did.'

'I probably ought to,' she replies. 'But I don't.'

'Because you like the idea of Lisa being shat on.'

'No. Not only that. Just – I don't know – what really happens in a relationship is hidden from everyone else. Only you two can judge what actually went on.'

'So?'

'So you just have to guess.'

'Guess what?'

'I've just . . . I've got faith in you. I know you and I know her, and from a position of total ignorance, I'm willing to say she got what she deserved.'

Guy slowly takes this in. 'I'm not sure I can agree with that,' he says, softly.

'Maybe I like you more than you like yourself,' Helen suggests.

Guy chuckles. 'That's what I always used to think about you,' he says.

Helen glances at her watch. 'We have to press on,' she says. 'We're not even half-way.'

'OK,' says Guy, getting up stiffly and shouldering his backpack. 'Whatever you say, boss.'

As they climb, sweating more than ever in the early afternoon sun, Guy feels a tide of happiness pulse through his body. Reaching a crest in the pass, a glimmer of ocean on the far side of the island – the east coast – winks through a narrow cleft in the valley ahead. Adjacent to this glimpse of the sea, perched on the northernmost mountain-top, is their destination: clean up against the sky, a tiny domed church, so perfectly white in this brown, thirsty landscape that it looks almost edible – an iced cake left behind by an out-of-scale picnic.

Prompted by Helen, Guy turns and sees that the west coast is now back in view – a generous expanse of the Aegean spread below, with a neat jigsaw-piece bay marking their starting-point. The houses in the town are now barely distinguishable white specks.

'Long way,' says Guy, proudly.

Helen nods. 'I'm so glad you came,' she says, with a swing of her arm which causes a couple of her fingers, perhaps accidentally, perhaps deliberately, to brush his hand.

'Obviously I'd rather be on the Piccadilly line at the moment,' he says. 'Preferably stuck between stations, ideally in a heatwave, but as a second choice this isn't so bad.'

They walk on, the path becoming steeper as they approach the church. Less tired now, as their goal approaches they gradually accelerate, the pain in their legs disappearing in the final push to the top of the hill.

In the church courtyard, a new and thrilling view opens up beneath them. From here, above a slope which descends to an immense cliff face, a giant, clear panorama of sea stretches unbroken for mile after mile towards its invisible join with a perfect, cloudless sky. Guy and Helen stare, lost in this blue universe – a pure, engulfing, featureless beauty of nothing more than scale and colour.

'You're dripping,' she says.

Guy smiles and wipes a palm across his forehead, bringing it away glistening with sweat.

'Let's go in,' says Helen. 'It'll be cooler.'

Stumbling over the loose stones – which, now, without a walking rhythm, seem hard to traverse – they circle the church to a concealed door which, inevitably, is painted blue. It is held shut by a length of wire twisted round a nail. Helen looks around, unsure if they are supposed to find someone to let them in, then untwists the wire and nudges open the door.

In silence they step inside, gazing at the dilapidated, seemingly abandoned interior – a surprise, given the church's pristine appearance from the outside. Three sides of the church are rough grey stone, unpainted and unadorned, with only the choir whitewashed. This whitewash fades away into a half-dome above the altar, revealing an ancient-looking fresco, largely crumbled away. All that is left of the image is the hands of two decapitated figures, their fingers pointing skywards, half a halo, and a smaller figure to one side – a balding man in a purple robe, giving what looks like a blessing with his right hand.

Aside from the fresco, the church is almost entirely bare, containing a few oil lamps and candles, a roughly made wooden screen holding some cheap modern icon-paintings and a wooden lectern on a concrete base, painted bright green. There is only one chair, with a plastic bag of kitchen roll hanging off the back.

They shuffle around the gritty stone floor, grateful for the cool air, and stand side by side, examining the strange fresco. Turning to face the emptiness of the church, Guy breaks the silence. 'Not a great spot for pulling a congregation,' he says, his voice echoing more loudly than he expected.

'I don't like it,' says Helen, stooping to examine a small plastic tub containing a few bright red nuggets of frankincense.

'Let's get out of here,' he replies, moving towards the sheet of sunlight slicing through the half-open doorway.

Helen follows, glancing back at the fresco, propelled outside by the odd sensation that the man in the purple robe has caught her eye.

Together, helping each other up, they climb the last few rocks up to the pinnacle of the mountain, where another dimension to the vista is suddenly added – rich, blue water now visibly surrounding them on three sides.

'This is incredible!' says Guy.

Helen nods, smiling, turning herself slowly round and round on the spot.

They sit, their legs touching, on a small flat rock at the very highest point on the island. A long, top-of-the-world silence sings between them, accompanied by the far-off clanking of a few goat bells and the barely audible swish of the seashore far below. Here, on this mountain peak, not speaking, Guy feels as if at last they are utterly together. The tension between them has been eased aside. Everything about the moment feels right.

'So,' he says, eventually. 'Are you going to tell me what happened?'

Squeezed together on their small rock, they are naturally looking away from one another, out to sea. Guy turns his head, waiting for a response, but Helen's face is unreadable. Her mouth doesn't move, her head doesn't turn, and her sunglasses, reflecting the sea and the sky, give nothing away. Guy waits, so long that he almost begins to wonder if he only imagined himself asking the question.

'Why did you go away?' he says.

Helen turns to Guy, bringing their faces uncomfortably close.

'Why do you want to know?' she asks, in a gentle, even tone, removing her shades and staring intently into his eyes.

'What?'

281

'Why do you want to know?'

'I'm your closest friend – you disappear for three months – I want to know.'

'Why?'

'Just . . .'

'Curiosity?'

'Partly . . .'

'Or you want to help?'

'Yes. I want to help.'

'Look at me.'

'What about you?'

'How do I look?'

'What do you mean?'

'I mean I'm fine. I don't need help. I sorted it out on my own. That's the whole point.'

'What whole point? The whole point of what?'

Helen twitches, brushing an insect from her thigh. 'Guy,' she says. 'I'm glad you're here. I'm very happy to see you. But everything's different now. I'm a different person.'

'I can see that.'

'I don't need help any more. I'm sorry, but . . . if that's what you came for, you've wasted your time. I don't want help.'

Guy takes this in, slowly.

'Good,' he says, after a while. 'That's good.'

They stare at one another, their silence once again filled with tension. Helen bows her head and looks away from Guy, down towards the sea. She sighs, emitting a hostile restlessness. She seems to want be on her own.

'Why?' he says. 'What happened?'

'It wasn't one thing, Guy. Or not just one thing. I can see now that I was depressed for a long time. I haven't been myself for years, and there was nothing anyone else could do about that. I'm grateful for all the support you gave me, but . . . it . . .'

'Didn't help.'

'No. It made me feel better, but it didn't help. Not really. It's funny – it's all so obvious now – but it was up to me. I couldn't face it on my own, though, because I was too depressed. Any help I got just prolonged the whole thing. It had to get worse before it could get better. And it did. Things got bad, and I thought I was going to crack up, and I ran away, and I ended up here, and . . . you know . . . on my own, away, things seemed different. A bit of space, a bit of time, and I've sorted things out. At least, I'm sort*ing* things out. It's not sudden. I didn't wake up one day and decide I was happy. I can just feel my trajectory's changed.'

Helen turns to look at Guy. He, too, twists to look at her. An almost apologetic smile forms on her lips. Guy smiles back, a thin, hard-to-decipher curl of his mouth. He doesn't speak.

'It's not being high or low that's important,' Helen says. 'It's whether you're going up or down.'

'And you're up,' says Guy, softly – almost inaudibly.

'Moving up. Moving up.'

'I can't believe you're saying this,' he says, his voice slightly louder.

'Why?'

'It's amazing.'

'Why?'

'Just . . . it's . . . the most fantastic thing I've ever heard.'

'You think so?'

'Of course it is.'

'Really?'

'What do you mean, "really?". Of course, really. You think I'm going to be upset that you feel better?'

'I don't know.'

'You think I preferred you depressed?'

'No. I was just a bit worried.'

'About what?'

'About what you'd say.'

'What did you *think* I'd say?'

'I don't know. I don't know.'

'I'm happy, Helen. It's superb.'

'I thought you might not be.'

'Of *course* I am.'

'Good,' she says. 'I'm happy you're happy.'

'No – I'm happy you're happy. I thought of it first.'

Helen laughs, and Guy's mind freezes, suddenly blank – swollen to capacity with the single, clear certainty that he loves her. Somehow, though, this thought feels inexpressible. More than ever, their friendship feels too strong – their closeness crystallizing ever more solidly without any flirtation or physicality. The closer she comes to him, the more powerfully and painfully this absence seems to gape between them.

He puts an arm around her back, giving her far shoulder an I'm-happy-you're-happy squeeze. She immediately responds, stretching an arm around his lower back. They sit, staring out to sea in silence, gently holding one another, but the rock they are sitting on is slightly too small, holding them at an awkward angle, and their arms begin to ache. They continue holding through the first glow of pain, then withdraw, not looking one another in the eye.

'I won't ask, then,' he says. 'What happened. If you ever want to tell me, I want to know, but if you don't want to tell me, that's fine.'

'It's not some massive secret, Guy. It's just a principle.'

'What principle?'

'That I can look after myself.'

'Don't take it too far, though,' he offers, with an odd lilt – phrasing it almost as a request.

'What do you mean?'

'Don't know. Nothing, really.'

'I won't,' says Helen, after a pause. She brushes his forearm for emphasis. 'I won't.'

He smiles, feeling suddenly tense.

'Are you going to stay here, then?' he says, slightly too loudly.

'Don't know.'

'Do they close up when summer ends?'

'Yeah.'

'But you might stay, anyway?'

'No. Not once they close.'

'You'll go home?'

'No.'

'Where, then?'

'Don't know.'

'What are you going to do?'

'Don't know.'

Guy looks at her, anxiously. 'Aren't you worried? Don't you need a plan?'

Helen slowly turns her face from the sea and peers at Guy, staring him down.

'What about you?' she says.

'What about me?'

'What are *you* going to do?'

He squints, not understanding the question.

'You're in the same position,' she says.

'Yeah?'

'You're not interested in your Ph.D. any more.'

He shrugs. 'I'll finish . . .'

'You don't want to be an academic.'

He shakes his head.

'You don't want to be a teacher.'

He shakes his head again, once, with the corners of his mouth turned down.

'So what are you going to do?'

He shrugs, and smiles.

'Don't know,' he says.

Helen smiles and shrugs back, raising her eyebrows in a small, friendly gloat. 'There you go, then,' she says. 'Same as me.'

'I have got one idea, though,' says Guy, his pulse suddenly accelerating.

'Of what you want to do?'

'No. Just . . . who I want to do it with.'

Under her tan Helen's face changes colour, flashing pale for a moment, then filling from the neck upwards with blood. She flinches, brushing a lock of hair back from her face.

'Who's that, then?' she says, her voice catching in her throat.

Guy hesitates a moment, then kisses her. Helen's lips against his feel strange – their incestuous, transgressive kiss ringing with the clatter of broken taboo – an end to their friendship that feels, oddly, not quite like the start of something else.

Helen's arm slowly reaches around his back, then suddenly jerks, grabbing him by a shoulder and pushing him away. He rises to his feet, startled, and stares at her. She fidgets, looking at him, looking out to sea, standing and sitting then almost immediately standing up again. Breathing heavily, she finally catches his eye.

'That's not a good idea,' she says, angrily. 'You shouldn't have done that.'

Guy's legs almost give way under him. 'Why?' he says.

'You know why.'

'I don't. I honestly don't.'

'We're friends,' she says. 'We're friends.'

'I thought you said everything's different.'

'Not everything, Guy. Not everything.'

'Why? Why can't we?'

'We just can't.'

'*Why?*'

'I'm still a fuck-up, Guy. I'm not ready.'

'Neither am I. I'm not ready. I'm a fuck-up, too. We can be fucked up together.'

'That's not funny.'

'It's not a joke. I'm serious. We don't have a choice. You can't pick the timing with things like this. It's happened, now. We can't go back.'

'I'm not ready.'

'So be ready. Make yourself ready. We can't just ignore it.'

'I want to ignore it. I'm not . . . It's too much of a risk. What about our friendship? You're all I've got.'

'You're all *I've* got. That's how it's supposed to be. It's what people spend their lives looking for. It doesn't happen twice. We're not going to find this with other people.'

'It's too much. If things go wrong, it would –. . .'

'We'll have to make sure they don't.'

'What if they do?'

'I don't think they will.'

'But they might.'

'You're saying you don't want to give it a try? You want me to go back home? You want me to leave?'

'No,' she says, her arm leaping up to grab him. 'No. No.' A cautious smile crawls across Helen's features. 'No,' she repeats.

'So what do we do?'

Helen takes Guy's hand and stares at him. Slowly, the space between them shrinks to nothing. In all the time they have spent together, in all their years of intimacy, he has never felt her body pressed up against his. They have hugged before, but never like this. His mind races with a bewildering, upsetting joy.

Helen pulls him closer, one hand cradling the back of his neck.

'Soon,' she whispers, her lips almost touching his ear. 'Soon. I need a bit more time. I'm sorry.'

She pulls back and examines Guy's face, anxiously. 'Is that enough? You won't leave?'

Guy folds his arms around her, his eyes clamping shut as he squeezes her against him, losing himself in the smell and the feel and the Helen-ness of Helen, sensing a weightlessness of vanished isolation as her bodily presence seems to merge with his, linking them in an understanding more profound than anything they have ever achieved with words.

They hold one another, dissolved together, all sense of time and space evaporating.

As sensation slowly returns to Guy's body and mind, he feels that Helen is crying in his arms, her body rippling in wave after wave of tiny convulsions. Only when she is finally still does he open his eyes.

Having almost forgotten where he was, the giant expanse of cobalt-blue sea, stretching unbroken to an invisible horizon, sparks against his eyes with a force of purity and surprise. He blinks, confused, as if waking up to bright sunshine unsure when or how he fell asleep.